an Island Reunion

CORAL ISLAND
BOOK SIX

LILLY MIRREN

black lab press

Epub ISBN: 978-1-922650-24-5

Paperback ISBN: 978-1-922650-25-2

Version 1.0

Published by Black Lab Press 2023

Lilly Mirren has asserted her right to be identified as the author of this Work in accordance with the Copyright, Designs and Patents Act 1988.

This is a work of fiction. Names, characters, organisations, places, events and incidents are either products of the author's imagination or are used fictitiously. Any resemblance to actual persons, living or dead, or actual events is purely coincidental.

Cover design by Erin D'Ameron Hill.

First published worldwide by Black Lab Press in 2023.

Brisbane, Australia.

www.blacklabpress.com

About An Island Reunion

Our Coral Island friends are having a school reunion. What could possibly go wrong?

It seems as though things in Taya's life are finally running smoothly, when she's faced with an unexpected tragedy that could bring her entire world crashing down around her.

Beatrice and Aidan take their dream trip around Europe to recover from the cafe disaster. When they return to the island, she throws herself into organising a high school reunion. But can she pull it all together in time?

Penny and Rowan must deal with the cracks in their relationship and find a way to cope with their differences as they navigate life as newlyweds. They'll discover that a happy marriage isn't as easy to nurture as they thought it would be.

It's been thirty years since the friends graduated from Coral Island State High School and the class is returning to the island to celebrate. But there will be more people at the reunion than were invited, and someone will leave in handcuffs.

When this group of friends finally solve the murder

mystery that has dogged them for decades, the revelations uncovered will shake them to the core.

Please note: this book is written using Australian English. Some words, spelling and phrases may be unfamiliar to you.

Read The Series In Order

CORAL ISLAND

One

AS THE CAR pulled into the circular driveway of her home, Beatrice Whitlock yawned. She covered her mouth then smiled at Aidan, who sat in the driver's seat.

"Glad to be home?" he asked.

She nodded. "We've had a fantastic six months abroad, but I'm grateful to be back on Coral Island. I'm ready to put my feet up and relax for a bit. Travelling is tiring."

Aidan laughed as the garage door rolled up and then accelerated gently into the garage. "What are you going to do first?"

"I have a few phone calls to make."

"Dani and Harry?"

"You know me well." Both her children were studying in Sydney, and she hadn't seen either one of them in three months since they both flew to Paris to spend a week with her and Aidan during their summer break.

Fudge, her adorable chocolate-coloured pug, and Nelly, Aidan's golden retriever, both bounded out of the vehicle. They'd stayed with Evie for the past six months, and she'd been teary when Bea and Aidan had arrived from the ferry to pick them up. Bea was glad to see the dogs after so long away.

She'd worried Fudge wouldn't remember her, but he was over-joyed to see her, licking all over her face. He'd slowed down somewhat, and there were some grey hairs around his face that hadn't been there when she left. It was a stark reminder that he was getting older and wouldn't be with them forever.

She and Aidan lugged their bags into the house, then up the stairs to their large master suite. Beatrice left everything outside the walk-in closet. She filled the dogs' bowls with water and food, then left them happily eating in the kitchen and headed for the shower. One entire wall of their bathroom was a large, glass panel that looked across the ocean. The shower wall shared the same view. As she took a shower, she watched seagulls diving and waves curling to shore along the empty beach.

The past six months had been a whirlwind of flights, hotels, walking trails, tourist destinations, and delicious food. She and Aidan had stopped in Hong Kong on the way to Europe, where they'd toured around much of the continent, then back via Phuket for a final two weeks at a beach resort before landing in Brisbane that morning.

They were both exhausted from the travel, but the entire trip had been the jaunt of a lifetime for them both. Bea had never felt so relaxed and happy. She and Aidan had spent almost every moment together and they'd enjoyed each other's company, tried new food, hiked various trails, and seen more sights than she could possibly remember. It was the kind of adventure she'd dreamed of having for so many years, and she'd finally been able to do it.

They'd sat in an olive grove to watch the sun set over Florence while sipping Chianti. They'd stood in line for hours to admire Michelangelo's *David*. They'd trekked part of the Camino de Santiago and eaten tapas at a small streetside café still bathed in sweat. They'd hiked the base of the Alps and gotten a tan on a beach in Nice. They'd eaten chocolate and dessert every single day. It'd been like a dream, and she'd shared it all with her one true love.

It was still surprising for her to believe that she'd ended up marrying her high school sweetheart, and that he was the down-to-earth, humble, and fun boy at heart she remembered him being even after so many years as a professional footballer. She had to pinch herself sometimes to remember it wasn't a fantasy but her reality.

Beatrice pulled on a velour strapless dress that felt more like a bathrobe than clothing and wandered into the kitchen to fix them both a snack. Aidan had brought in the two bags of groceries they'd purchased on the way home, and set them on the kitchen bench. She poured two glasses of cold iced tea and sliced cheese to sit on top of crackers alongside a handful of olives. Then she took everything out onto the deck to wait for Aidan.

With her feet up on another chair, she leaned back and relaxed, taking in the view. It was good to be home. Even though this house had been Aidan's before they were married, he hadn't lived there long, so she'd been able to make it theirs in the short time they'd spent before their trip away. Sometimes she missed the cottage, but now that Charmaine had moved in, she could visit whenever she liked without disturbing the tenant. She was grateful to be able to help her friend get more settled on the island after everything that had happened with Charmaine's brother.

Even thinking about Sean set her nerves jangling. She hoped he never came back. Perhaps the police had found him, although she was sure her friends would've mentioned that in one of the dozens of emails they'd sent her while she was away.

She picked up her phone and dialled Harry's number. He answered right before she hung up, sounding sleepy.

"Are you napping in the middle of the day?" she asked with a laugh.

He grunted. "Mum?"

"I'm back on Coral Island."

"That's great, Mum. I'm glad you're back. I can't wait to see you." He sounded tired, but happy.

"It's been a long time. I'm looking forward to one of your hugs."

He laughed. "Will you come to Sydney?"

"I have no desire to set foot on a plane for a while, but maybe you can come here during your next break. Or over a weekend."

"Okay, that's fine. If you're paying, I'll come next week. I miss you."

"That's wonderful—I'm so excited. I'll pay, and I'll even throw in a few home-cooked meals. How are your classes going?"

He sighed. "Medicine is harder than I thought it'd be. There's so much to learn."

She imagined him running his long, agile fingers through the dark curls that flopped across his forehead again the moment he let them go. "It's difficult, but I know you can do it. You've always been able to tackle anything you wanted."

"Thanks, Mum, but that doesn't make me feel better. It puts more pressure on me. I can't handle any more pressure."

"Fine," she replied. "No pressure. I won't say anything except I love you and miss you. I'm looking forward to seeing you soon."

"You too, Mum."

She hung up the phone and then called Danita. She'd managed to convince her daughter to remain in the interior design degree she'd been enrolled in for the previous two years. Danita was in her third year of studies and had resisted her boyfriend's urging to switch to architecture, at least for now.

"Hi, Mum," Danita said in her patented busy tone of voice.

"Are you in the middle of something?"

"I have an assignment due, and I'm running a little late, so I'm typing like a madwoman. Are you home?"

"I'm home!"

"That's great, Mum. I'm looking forward to seeing you. We both are."

"Both? You mean you and Harry?"

Bea could almost hear the eye roll. "No, Mum. Me and Damien. We're living together now, remember?"

How could Bea forget? Her beautiful, young university student had moved in with one of her professors. A man who eschewed furniture for cushions and who liked to reject Bea's cooking — something she had yet to forgive.

"Oh, yes, of course. Well, I can't wait to see you. Harry's coming up next weekend. Do you want to come then too? My treat."

"We'd love to. My assignments will be done by then, and that's exactly the break we need."

Bea's heart sank. The invitation hadn't been intended to include Damien, although she supposed that was how her daughter travelled now. With a middle-aged professor in tow. She bit down on her lip — her attitude was going to cause friction with Dani. She had to pull herself together and learn to accept this intruder into her family whether she liked him or not. Aidan had warned her not to drive Dani away, but it was so difficult to hold her tongue. She'd spent two decades telling her daughter how to live, and now she should disapprove in silence?

After she hung up the phone with Dani, she wandered inside to see where Aidan was. The cheese was getting shiny, and the crackers would be stale if he didn't hurry. She called out to him, but there was no response. Perhaps he was in the shower.

Her laptop sat on the bench beside a pile of unopened

mail. She'd tackle the mail later. Instead, she picked up her laptop and carried it back out to the deck, where she fired it up. There were dozens of unread email messages. She hadn't kept up-to-date with her emails while she was away. She'd taken the laptop but had only replied to the urgent messages, since they'd kept so busy touring, walking, and eating out.

Suddenly, a slew of emails filtered into her updating inbox with the same subject line.

RE: RSVP for the Reunion!

She froze, her heart hammering against her ribcage. The reunion. She'd forgotten all about it. Before she went away, she'd thought it would be a great idea to put together a reunion for Coral Island High. It'd been thirty years since she, Taya, Evie, Penny, Rowan, and Aidan had graduated from high school, and she thought they should celebrate.

But now the reunion was only a couple of months away, and she hadn't done anything about it other than sending out the initial save-the-date invitation. There were at least thirty RSVPs in her inbox. How had she missed them before now? The entire event had slipped her mind. If she was going to go through with it, there was so much to organise before the date rolled around. She wasn't sure she could manage it.

Or if she even wanted to.

What was the point of bringing together a bunch of people she hadn't seen since high school? The people she cared about still lived on the island—well, most of them. Penny and Rowan were itinerant now, going where his job took him all over the world. But the others were still here, and she could see them any time she liked. Did she want to see the other high school graduates who'd run away from the island and hadn't looked back?

Aidan sat down at the table with her and reached for his glass with a sigh. "It's hot."

"I forgot how hot it gets here, and it's nearly winter." She laughed and raised her glass. "Let's toast to being home."

"Home sweet home," he said, clinking his glass against hers with a wink. His hair was wet, and he wore a pair of board shorts that hung low around his waist and no T-shirt. She loved being married to him; she could stare as much as she liked.

"I'm enjoying you back in board shorts," she said.

He laughed. "Not as much as I'm enjoying your little sundress."

She squinted at the computer screen as the flood of emails brought her back to the moment. "Do you remember me saying I was going to arrange a school reunion?"

He reached for a cracker with cheese. "Mmmm."

"I sent out the invitation before we left."

He arched an eyebrow. "You did? For what date?"

"The eighth of July."

"This year?" He took a bite of cracker.

"Yes, this year. In two months. I can't believe I did that, knowing we were going away."

"I'm sure you thought you could manage it."

"I believe my thinking was that I'd delegate while I was away, but I forgot all about it. We were having too much fun. And now I have no one to help me, and no idea what we're going to do. I mean, I suppose we could all meet at the *Surf and Sea* for dinner, but that's boring. And when you get a whole bunch of people around a long table, no one gets to talk to anyone other than the people seated right next to them. It's not a great way to catch up after so much time." She chewed on a fingernail. "I don't know. Maybe I should talk to Evie and Taya. They're bound to have better ideas than that."

"I think that's probably wise. And what about Chaz? She was great at planning our wedding. Maybe she can help too."

"That's brilliant," Bea said, perking up immediately. "Chaz can help with it."

Aidan laughed. "But it's not her reunion, so you can't dump it on her."

"I'm not saying she should pull the whole thing together, but so long as it's not *all* on my shoulders. I'm tired—we've had a busy six months. And besides, I can't remember why I wanted to plan it in the first place. I'm going to call Chaz and ask her to be my party planner."

"Speaking of the future," Aidan said, "have you thought about what you'd like to do now that the café is gone?"

Bea swallowed. She had thought about it, but she was nervous. Not about what Aidan would think of her idea, but about whether it made any sense. Could she handle it?

"I'd like to go back to university," she said. "I never finished my degree all those years ago, and I'd like to do that."

"Weren't you studying accounting or something?"

"Business," she said. "I might've ended up in accounting, but I hadn't decided yet. Still, I don't think that's what I'll study this time around. I'm thinking of studying food science."

"I didn't know that was a degree," Aidan said, "but it sounds perfect for you."

"It may not lead to a job. I have no idea. But you know how much I love food, and I like the idea of studying nutrition and the process of food development from the moment the seed is planted in the ground until it's eaten and then how the body processes and uses it for energy. There's so much value in nutrition. It can make our bodies healthy or sick, it can heal us or make us worse, it can give us good mental health or bad. I don't think there's enough emphasis on it, and I'd like to get a better understanding of it all."

Aidan reached for her hand and squeezed it. "That would be amazing, and exactly the kind of thing you'd enjoy doing. I say go for it."

"You don't mind that I won't be earning any money, and it may not result in me having a career at the end of it? I mean, I hope it does, but I don't know how many jobs are out there in the field of food science. It's not exactly mainstream."

Aidan shrugged. "It doesn't matter to me. We have plenty to live on for the rest of our lives. I only teach PE because I like it. I won't be earning until next year either, although I'm going to check on a real estate development I've got going over in Blue Shoal later today. I've been slack in following up with the builder, and the project has practically ground to a halt."

Bea wanted to squeal with delight. Instead, she climbed into Aidan's lap and kissed him softly on the mouth. "I'm so grateful for you."

She still wasn't accustomed to having a husband who supported her choices no matter what they might be, but she would never stop being thankful for him and for the second chance they'd had to find each other and spend their lives together.

Two

CHARMAINE BILLINGS WAS twenty-seven years old. She'd moved past her mid-twenties with a rush of nervous energy and family crises, and now she was headed for her late twenties. How did she get here? And so quickly. She stared at her reflection in the bathroom mirror at the beach cottage she'd rented from Beatrice six months earlier. She poked and prodded at her face, noting the new laugh lines around her mouth and the crow's feet beginning to make an appearance beside her eyes. This was not good.

"I'm old," she whispered to herself, at which point her face turned bright red and she wanted to laugh. It was ridiculous to consider herself old at twenty-seven, but she couldn't help it. She wasn't used to being an adult, let alone someone approaching thirty. Apart from the fact that she finally had a long-term job and had rented her very own cottage by the beach, she didn't feel much like an adult. Although, she supposed she was more adult-like than she had ever been in her life before, so at least she was heading in the right direction.

She even had a steady boyfriend, something she'd previously thought would be impossible for her, given her shyness. But Bradford was still in her life, astounding her every day with his ability not only to stick around but to treat her like a princess. She didn't quite know how to handle it, but she was growing used to that as well.

With a glance at her watch and a rush of nerves that formed a ball in her gut, she realised she was going to be late. She threw on a dash of lip balm, ran her fingertips over her crazy eyebrows to calm them down, and hurried for the door. Her cat, Watson, sat bathing himself in a puddle of sunshine on the kitchen floor. He looked up at her lazily as she rushed past.

"Bye, Watson. Make sure to take care of the place while I'm gone."

She grinned to herself — she truly believed that if Bradford ever dumped her, she would end up a cat lady, surrounded by felines and talking to them as if they were her children. But she could imagine worse fates, so the prospect didn't particularly scare her. What could be better than a bevy of cats preening and washing themselves or curling up in her lap at night while she painted at her easel?

Finn, her aunt and Watson's official owner, had gifted her the cat when she moved into the cottage as a housewarming present.

"He's practically yours anyway. We hardly ever see him," she'd said as she handed him over in a travel cage. "He'll probably find his way back to town, but anyway, you can see if he'll stay with you at the cottage."

And he had stayed. He'd never missed spending a night with her and seemed to love the beach lifestyle. She'd bought him a collar with a bell so the wildlife could stay out of his reach, but he spent most of his time wandering around near the sand and then throwing himself down into a warm patch to sleep.

It didn't take her long to ride her bike into town, although she was bathed in sweat by the time she got there. It was her day off, and she'd agreed to meet the girls for brunch at a new casual dining place called *Ambience* down by the dock in Kellyville. It wasn't the same as a trip to *Bea's Coffee* had been, and she missed the café terribly. But she'd decided to give the new establishment a chance. After all, where could they meet for brunch otherwise?

She climbed off the bike in front of the restaurant and bumped the tyres up over the gutter, then leaned it on the bike rack. No need to lock it up, since nothing bad ever happened on Coral Island. Unless, of course, her brother visited. Then all bets were off.

With a shiver as the memory of his last stay on the island washed over her, she hugged herself briefly before stepping into the cool, air-conditioned, cosy restaurant. Bea, Taya, and Evie were seated in the back section in a corner away from the few other diners. Bea waved to Charmaine, and she waved back, then strode to meet them.

She kissed their cheeks, then took the only remaining seat across from Bea.

"It's good to see you, Chaz," Evie said. "We need your advice as an event planner. Bea wants us to have the reunion at a restaurant."

"I don't *want* us to have it at a restaurant. It's simply the only thing I could think of," Bea protested with a shake of her head. Her blonde bob grazed her tanned shoulders, and she crossed her arms over her chest.

"I think we should go scuba diving," Evie said. "We could hire one of Bradford's yachts."

"Scuba diving?" Taya blanched. "I'm afraid of the ocean."

"You live on an island!" Evie blurted.

Taya's cheeks reddened. "I know—I mean, the deep ocean.

13

I can swim and snorkel in the shallows, but I think the deeper parts are spooky."

Charmaine listened to the back-and-forth banter for a few minutes before interjecting. "Scuba diving might be a bit intense for some people, and a restaurant could be a touch tame for others."

Bea shrugged. "Any other ideas, then?"

"What about a scavenger hunt?" Charmaine offered.

The ladies looked unconvinced.

"A scavenger hunt? I don't know." Bea fidgeted with a napkin.

"Isn't that a bit childish?" Evie asked.

Taya sucked her cheeks in, but didn't say anything.

The waiter came to take their orders and disappeared again, leaving them to continue their conversation. The break had given Charmaine a chance to gather her thoughts. The more she thought about it, the more she liked the idea.

"Bear with me, ladies. We could have an adult scavenger hunt and make it fun. The clues could lead to drinks or challenges, and we could make sure everyone gets to interact. We can use the challenges for people to find out things about each other, since it's been so long since everyone's gotten together."

"It's not a bad idea," Bea replied. "We could make one of the challenges how many people you can recognise."

"Like a facial recognition bingo," Taya added, laughing.

"That would be fun," Evie admitted. "I'll bet I'd win that one."

"My memory is terrible," Bea said. "I've probably forgotten everyone."

They talked about their teenaged antics and who they remembered doing what from those years. There was the time that Rowan had hidden the school mascot on the roof and then climbed up to retrieve it and broken his arm when he fell to the ground. An incident involving the entire football team and a dozen cream pies was forever seared in each of their memories. And the moment Bea found out about her mother's death — that was something they'd never forget. She'd stood there, silent and still, according to her friends, until she'd spun on her heel and ran from the school grounds. Charmaine was glad she hadn't been there as a witness, her heart clenched at the thought of it.

She pulled out a folder as the waiter returned with their meals. She had ordered scrambled eggs on toast with bacon and avocado, Bea had a plate of waffles with ice cream, and Evie's plate was stacked with pancakes and buttery syrup. Taya had ordered an açai bowl topped with sliced fresh fruit.

Charmaine set the folder on the table next to her plate and made notes. "We don't have to go with a scavenger hunt, but I'll jot it down as an idea and we can each think about it some more and see how it feels the next time we get together."

"That sounds good," Bea said.

"Phew. At least we might have one part of the reunion planned." Evie drew a deep breath. "Bea, when you called and asked me to help with the event, I honestly wasn't sure what I could do. I'm not very good at party planning. The biggest thing I've planned is my book club, and that's usually basic."

"Between the four of us, we'll come up with something special," Taya said. "I'm looking forward to it."

"Do you think anyone will attend?" Evie asked, then sipped her cappuccino.

Bea swallowed a mouthful of waffles. "I've already got around thirty RSVPs — about half were negative, but the rest said yes. So, unless they back out at the last minute, they're coming to Coral Island on the eighth of July. There's the four of us and our plus-ones, Penny and Rowan... I think we'll have a pretty good turnout. It won't be the whole class, but it'll be close. Everyone has replied, including our teachers and the principal who ran the school at the time."

"Principal McDermott? Is he coming?" Taya asked.

"No. He's living in an aged care facility. His daughter emailed to let me know he's thinking of us, but he won't be able to make it."

"Oh, that's a shame," Evie said. "I always liked him."

"There was something else I wanted to talk to you about while I have you all together," Charmaine said. She wasn't sure where to start. It'd been six months since she'd overheard Betsy and Frank's conversation at the florist shop where she worked. She hadn't mentioned a word of it to anyone before now. The reasoning wasn't clear in her mind — she wasn't entirely sure what any of it meant.

She couldn't believe that her boss and friend could be capable of doing anything particularly bad, since she was such a nice person. And maybe she'd misunderstood their conversation. Besides, they were angry—at least, Frank was, and who says exactly what they mean when they're in that kind of emotional state?

But keeping the information to herself had taken a toll. She'd begun to feel anxious whenever she saw her friends, or when she was at work and Betsy acted strangely about something. Or even when she watched the news. It didn't make sense, but she was ready to try anything to achieve some peace in her life — something she'd only managed to achieve for a short while before her brother's visit to Coral Island had thrown everything into disarray.

"What is it?" Bea asked before biting into a forkful of waffles.

"Before you went away, I overheard a conversation between Betsy and her son. I was outside the shop, about to go in, when I was stopped by shouting. It was Frank yelling at Betsy. I didn't want to interfere or embarrass them—and besides, I hate confrontations—so I sat outside and leaned my ear up against the glass." She blushed. "I wasn't snooping. I wanted to know when it was over so I could go in."

"Of course you weren't snooping. We know that," Taya encouraged her. "What happened next?"

"I'd printed out some articles we found about the kidnapping. That woman, Betsy Alton, in California who was wanted for taking her son out of the state — do you remember?"

All three women nodded, their breakfasts forgotten momentarily as they listened, transfixed.

"Frank came into the shop when I was looking at the articles, and he must've seen them. He confronted her about it—said he believed the articles were about him and Betsy. That he was the kidnapped boy."

"Why didn't you say anything about this before now?" Taya asked.

Charmaine swallowed hard. Was she doing the right thing? Her stomach churned. It felt as though she was betraying her friend. "I didn't want to stab Betsy in the back. She's been so good to me, like a second mother. She takes care of me and is kind. She knows I have the articles, Frank told her, but she hasn't said a thing to me about it. I think she did what she had to do to protect herself and Frank. She said her husband was a dangerous man, that he treated them badly and she had no choice but to leave. Then she told Frank that his father looked for them until he died. She seemed afraid."

"That makes sense," Evie admitted. "If it was her—and it sounds like she admitted as much—then Betsy Alton must've come to Coral Island to escape her past and changed her name. I wonder why her brother came too."

"Maybe they wanted to stick together," Bea suggested.

"There's more," Charmaine said, her fingers drumming on the tabletop. "She said Buck was innocent of Mary's murder."

"Well, that's not news," Taya said, her lips turning down at the corners. "She's always claimed he didn't do it."

"Yes, but she said something else interesting. She said that the police only believe he was the murderer because she wanted them to."

Three

THE BRUNCH DATE with her friends troubled Taya Eldridge as she walked back to her car. She sat in the driver's seat and slipped her feet out of the heels she always wore and into a pair of comfortable sandals she kept in the car for driving. A quick check in the mirror showed that her red lipstick needed a touch-up after eating the açai bowl, and she smoothed her hair down before reaching for her purse.

If Betsy was somehow involved in framing her own brother for a murder she knew he didn't commit, why would she spend decades declaring his innocence and even pay his exorbitant bail fee? It didn't make any sense, unless she was a conniving criminal mastermind who'd planned the whole thing. But then, what would her motive be for something like that? No, there must be some other more reasonable explanation for what Chaz had overheard that day. If she'd believed it at the time, she would've said something before now. But she hadn't. She'd kept it to herself and even now didn't seem particularly convinced of her own theory.

Taya started the car and began the drive back to Blue Shoal, where she lived and where her old inn still sat perched above the small cove with a view of the village and the new resort her father had built. She worked for him now, traveling all over Asia and the Pacific to bring each resort up to the standard her father had always maintained for his resorts. He'd confided in her a few weeks earlier that he was getting too old to travel as much as he had, and he'd hoped she would take over the business soon so he could spend his remaining years with her mother.

It was hard for her to grasp the concept of Cameron Eldridge slowing down. Most of her childhood years were spent waiting for him to come through the front door to throw the ball with her or to take her swimming—things other people's fathers did, but hers rarely showed up for. Still, he loved her, and she knew that. It wasn't the number of hours they spent together that counted, but the quality of that time.

The realisation of the truth in that statement hadn't been something she could appreciate until more recently. For most of her teen years and her twenties, she'd resented him greatly for being absent so often. But they'd reconciled recently, and she went to dinner at her childhood home every time she was back from her travels.

The drive back to Blue Shoal was a pleasant one since the roadwork had been completed the previous year. Each rainy season brought new potholes, but so far, the council had managed to fix them before any vehicles disappeared into their depths, so it seemed as though the road might stay in good shape—unlike the track that'd crossed the island before it.

She drove past the Blue Shoal Inn, the boutique hotel she and her husband had owned together before he passed from cancer so many years earlier. It still looked fantastic after the facelift she'd given it before she sold it to her father's company, Paradise Resorts. The usual twang of guilt in her stomach over selling the place didn't eventuate as she passed the property, and she wondered if perhaps she'd finally cut the ties between the quaint old inn and her heart.

The parking space outside her office at Paradise Resort Coral Island had her name on a sign at one end. She pulled her sports car into the space and cut the engine. She'd been nervous to work at her father's company, but so far, she'd had a positive experience.

Everyone had been very welcoming—no one seemed concerned about her stepping on toes. She'd grown as a businessperson and as an individual in the short time she'd been there. The role she'd taken on was a challenging one, but it gave her the opportunity to get to know each resort intimately and to understand the staff personally. It was an invaluable way to learn about the business before her father handed it over, although she still didn't feel qualified to take on that role since she hadn't been there long enough, and her father had a natural gift for business she wasn't certain she'd inherited.

"Good afternoon, Miss Eldridge," Susan said in a chipper voice, her amber curls pulled into a messy bun. As Taya's assistant, Susan had made herself invaluable over recent months, helping Taya stay on top of what was going on in the office whenever she travelled.

"Good afternoon, Susan. Any messages?"

"They're on your desk."

"Wonderful. Thank you."

"You have a meeting at two o'clock with Mr Reddy."

"Oh, I forgot about that. Thanks for the reminder." Taya shut her office door and inhaled a quick breath. There was never a lack of things to do or people to meet with, but since she'd been dating Andrew Reddy for over a year, she was grateful for every opportunity to see him, even if they did have to remain professional.

She sat at her desk and slipped her purse into the bottom drawer. Then she flicked on the computer monitor and got to work thinning out the urgent emails in her inbox. Whenever she stepped away from her computer for more than an hour, the unread messages piled up. There had to be a better way of organising them, but she honestly didn't have the time to figure it out. When things slowed down . . . She shook her head. She said that a lot.

When things slowed down, she'd look for a new house. When things slowed down, she'd take a trip with her friends for pleasure instead of for work. When things slowed down, she'd go on that cruise with her parents they always talked about — they'd already booked themselves tickets on a ship that sailed from Vancouver to Alaska and back again. They were extremely excited; they planned on spending several weeks in Alaska before taking the return trip. They'd asked her repeatedly to join them, but she couldn't see how she could manage a month-long holiday at this early stage in her career.

When she'd said that, her father had replied, "Don't let it bog you down, sweetie. The company exists for you. You don't exist for it."

She'd rolled her eyes at that. "You haven't exactly practiced what you're preaching, Dad."

He'd kissed her cheek. "Learn from my mistakes. Don't repeat them."

"Yes, Dad. Okay, fine—I'll book the ticket as soon as I can. Let me check my calendar with Susan first."

The memory prompted Taya to press the intercom connecting her phone to Susan's. "Hi. Can you please call my mum to find out the dates for their cruise and then check them against my calendar? I don't see how I can possibly manage four weeks away, but I told them I'd try to figure it out."

"No worries. I'll get that information for you right away."

"Thank you." How would she manage any of it without Susan? It'd taken her a while to grow accustomed to having an assistant, but now she found herself asking for help more and more often.

Half an hour later, she'd made a dent in her inbox, but there was still a long way to go. She sighed and ran her fingers through her hair, blinking rapidly. She should blink more. The computer screen was giving her a headache. Or perhaps she finally needed reading glasses. She'd avoided addressing it for as long as she could manage, straining to read, putting up with the headaches, not wanting to go down that path. But it was no doubt inevitable. Both her parents wore glasses, and she was bound to find herself in the same position eventually.

There was a knock at her office door.

"Come in," she called.

Andrew opened the door and walked in. She rose to greet him, and they kissed. He linked his arms around her waist, and she wound hers around his neck.

"How are you?" he asked.

She blinked again. "Tired. My eyes are worn out from that screen."

"You should ask Susan to book you an eye appointment."

"You're probably right." She sighed. "I'm getting old."

"Happens to the best of us," he said softly, leaning in to kiss her lips again.

She stepped out of his embrace to check her calendar. "I thought we were meeting at two."

"We are. I came a little early because I missed you and wanted to see you."

"I won't object to that," she replied, moving back into his arms.

Her phone rang. She should pick it up—shouldn't ignore it. She was at work, after all. But Andrew's lips were soft, his presence intoxicating. She felt it from the tips of her toes, all the way up into her head, which was spinning as though she'd inhaled too quickly. The ringing stopped, then started up again.

"I should get that," she whispered, pulling away.

Andrew kissed her neck lightly. "I'm sure they can wait."

"It could be important."

"You're the boss," he said.

"Not yet. Dad's still in charge, and he doesn't like it when I don't answer my phone." With a laugh, she extricated herself from his arms and reached for the phone. "Hello?"

"Honey, it's Mum." Her mother's shaking voice made her breath stick in her throat. "Your dad's had a heart attack. Come home."

She couldn't recall what happened next. The things she said to her mother before hanging up, the frantic search for where she'd stowed her purse. The stumbling over Andrew's feet as she hurried past him and out the door.

"Where are you going?" he called after her. "What's happened?"

"Home. Dad's unwell," she said. She couldn't say more. Andrew might be her boyfriend, but this business was her father's. The last thing he'd want was for her to send the employees into a panic.

She was so lightheaded that she couldn't find her parking space even though it was the closest one to her office. When her eyes lit on the red sports car, she ran to it and jumped in, then sped away on the small, winding road that led to her parents' mansion.

Her heart thudded against her ribcage. This couldn't be happening. Her father was fit, healthy, and not very old. Almost seventy, but not yet. Her parents had her young. After she was born, they'd tried but had never been able to get pregnant again, something they'd likely grieved. Still, they'd never let her see their grief, always treating her as though she was the one child they'd wanted and was everything they could've hoped for.

She'd been an ungrateful teen, rebellious and smart-mouthed. It wasn't until her own husband died when they were still young, leaving her alone, a single mother, that she'd begun to appreciate her parents and how much they'd done for her, how well they'd loved her.

Dad had worked too hard for too long. He was semi-retired and looking forward to spending time with his wife. He deserved to rest after all he'd built and the hours he'd logged. He couldn't die. It wouldn't be fair for him—for any of them. They were going on a cruise...

The drive to her parents' house was quick. They lived close by in the large stone house where she'd spent her childhood. She pulled the car into the circular driveway, but she was stopped by the presence of an ambulance parked outside the front door. The large oak door was swung wide, but there was no sign of anyone about. With a yank at the steering wheel, she turned the vehicle to park it outside the large garage. Then she climbed out and dashed across the lawn to the side door, which her mother always left unlocked.

Inside, she heard voices. She climbed the staircase to the master suite and found her mother pacing the bedroom.

"Taya. There you are," Mum said, hurrying to meet her and taking both hands to squeeze them, then released them again. "He's gone, honey. He's gone. I can't believe it." Mum buried her face in her hands and sobbed loudly.

Taya stood gaping, her throat closing over. "No, no, no... Where is he? Mum! Where is he?"

Mum pointed at the bathroom, and Taya ran. She found two paramedics raising a gurney with her father strapped to it. He was ashen and didn't look like himself. It sent a shiver through her body. Goose bumps prickled down her arms, and she fought the urge to scream.

"Dad," she whispered, taking his hand. It was still warm, but there was no life in it, no response. Usually he'd embrace her so hard, it sent the breath wheezing from her lungs. Then he'd laugh and pat her back, telling her to toughen up. But instead, he lay still, all his colour drained away.

"Can't you do something?"

The paramedics shook their heads and offered their condolences, but they stepped aside to give her a moment alone with her father. She stood there, helpless, holding his hand. Tears streamed down her cheeks.

"It's too soon, Dad. You were meant to enjoy your retirement years with Mum. It's not fair for you or for her. You were going to travel, to have fun — finally, after all these years of work. I'm not ready to take over the company." Panic flooded her mind as the realisation dawned. "No, you can't leave me yet. I've still got so much to learn. I don't want to destroy your legacy, and I'm not prepared."

She stood with her mother's hand on her shoulder. They watched as Dad was rolled away on the gurney. Taya's tears had stopped, but the pain in her throat grew by the moment. Her life would never be the same again.

Four

PLANS for the reunion were coming together better than Beatrice had thought they would. She was very grateful for Chaz, Taya and Evie. Penny had offered to help, but Bea had pointed out that she wasn't sure how much help she could be from Paris. Penny had agreed, but had assured Bea she and Rowan would be back on Coral Island in time for the reunion. She didn't want to miss it, since she felt like she'd already missed out on so much. But Bea had reassured her that nothing had changed on the island, and she'd been away for half a year anyway, so Penny hadn't missed anything.

Bea was parked at the ferry terminal waiting for her children to walk over the gangplank and onto Coral Island for the weekend. Plus, of course, Dani's boyfriend. A fact Bea was happy to forget, but forgetting wouldn't change anything. She and Aidan had talked about it and decided that the best thing for them to do would be not to offend Dani or her professor, that the relationship would likely take its own course towards a natural end when Dani, who was a very clever girl, would rightly conclude that the two of them had nothing in common.

It was a risky plan, but Bea didn't know what else to do. If she confronted her daughter and told her what she thought, Dani's stubborn streak might surface, and she could end up staying with the cushion-buying, tunic-wearing, shisha-smoking architect to spite them.

When Harry stepped off the ferry and onto dry land, Bea climbed from the car and waved above her head. Danita and Damien followed Harry hand in hand. Damien looked even smaller and older than she'd remembered.

Behave.

She said the word softly beneath her breath, reminding herself that there was a lot at stake. Her daughter no longer had a legal obligation to live beneath her roof or listen to what she had to say. She should be cautious. But still, all she wanted to do was shout that he was not the man for Dani and if he didn't leave immediately, she'd shove that pipe he loved directly...

"Welcome back to Coral Island," she called, striding to meet the three of them.

She embraced them one at a time, kissing cheeks and remarking over how thin Harry was or how tanned Dani had become. Her beautiful daughter had dyed her naturally blonde hair a brownish colour, but she bit her tongue to keep from remarking on it. She still looked stunning. There was no getting around how pretty her face was, but it was a shame she'd changed her hair. Bea had always loved its golden shine. It reminded her of the three-year-old who'd laughed at life and spent hours swinging in the park with Bea patiently pushing until her legs almost went up over her head. Still, she'd shouted, *higher!*

"You look good, Mum," Dani said as she lifted her luggage into the boot of the car. "It's only been three months since I've seen you, but you seem rested."

"You all look fantastic," Bea replied. "Now, let's get going.

I've got some cakes for you to try. I don't have a bakery anymore, so I'm always cooking something, and Aidan says if I don't stop, I'm going to make him fat, so the three of you will need to bring your appetites with you."

* * *

Aidan was waiting to make coffee when they arrived at the house. Both dogs bounded around in excitement until Bea finally gave them each a treat to chew and shooed them away. They all sat out on the deck and ate scones with jam and cream, banana cake, chocolate mud cake with caramel ganache, and freshly sliced fruit arranged on a white platter with a big blue dolphin painted along one side.

"Phew. It's good to be back on the island," Dani said with a loud sigh. "I've missed this place, although I'm still getting used to you not living in the cottage."

"I know. It's so strange that there's a renter living there," Harry added, his brow furrowed. "I hope they're taking care of it."

"She's taking very good care of it, and her name is Chaz. She's a friend of mine. I trust her completely."

"Isn't she the one whose brother burned down your café?" Dani asked around a mouthful of scone.

Damien looked alarmed. "What?"

"Allegedly," Bea corrected her. "We don't know that for sure. And it's not her fault she has a sociopathic brother. We all have our burdens to bear." She did her best not to look at Damien, instead focusing her attention on slicing a small piece of mud cake to slide onto her plate.

"Well, I don't know if you should have a friend like that," Dani continued. "She sounds dangerous, Mum. And I worry about you. We both do."

"You and Harry?" Bea asked.

"Me and Damien," Dani replied with a huff. "You're doing all sorts of strange things lately. Making friends with people related to murderers and arsonists. Damien says that for a small island, there are certainly a lot of felons living here, and I'd have to agree. What's going on?"

Bea and Aidan exchanged a glance. He arched an eyebrow as if to remind her to be nice. Why did he think she needed a reminder? She was always nice. Manners were one of the things she'd never struggled with. As long as she'd been an adult, she'd always managed to act perfectly respectable in public, even if she seethed beneath the surface.

She raised her chin and turned back to the task of eating her cake. The chocolate was deliciously rich, not too sweet, and the cake was moist and heavy. Exactly how she liked her mud cake. She could think about cake instead of her daughter's words and the boyfriend who was putting ideas in her head. He never seemed to speak the words himself, instead using Dani as a mouthpiece.

"It sounds like you've blown things a little out of proportion," Aidan replied. "Coral Island is completely safe. Nothing terrible happens here... at least not most of the time. Accidents are part of life, and according to the police, the fire is likely to have been an accident. They've completed their investigation, but still haven't managed to interview Sean. When they do, they'll no doubt find he wasn't involved, but even if he was, at least he's no longer on the island. The police will figure it out and make sure justice is served, however that looks."

Bea nodded. "Now, who would like more cake?"

Five

THE FOLLOWING SATURDAY, Charmaine found herself seated on a small yacht near Point Prospect, wearing a one-piece red bathing suit, a cotton cover-up, a large floppy straw hat, and oversized sunglasses. She lounged back on the deck and adjusted the pillow beneath her head.

"You're spoiling me," she said lazily.

Bradford laughed, handing her a champagne flute. "You deserve it."

"But I didn't do anything."

"Yes, you did. You're always so good to me, I thought it was about time I returned the favour. Besides, you work so hard every day between the florist's, wedding planning, and now the reunion, I thought it would be a good idea to give you a break."

Charmaine sat up straight so she could sip her champagne. "Mmmm... Thank you. It does feel good to relax. I've been spending every spare moment I have on weddings and party planning. There was a gap in the market when I decided to take on Penny and Rowan's wedding, and now word is spreading across the island that I'm affordable."

"And very good at your job. Maybe you should raise your rates."

Her cheeks flushed with warmth. "Thank you. And I'm sure you're right. If I charged more, I could do fewer parties and spend more time with you."

"I approve the plan wholeheartedly," Bradford replied with a grin.

Bradford wore a white shirt, unbuttoned, and a pair of blue board shorts. His hair was mussed and shoved beneath a peaked cap. He was tanned and fit, and he stepped around the boat on bare feet, adjusting ropes and pulling on this and that. Charmaine didn't know any of the technical terms, but she imagined they were jibs and sails or something equally impressive-sounding. She watched him in silence, sipping her champagne.

Behind Bradford stretched the sparkling azure waters of the Pacific Ocean. Sunlight danced on the water's surface, the shallow waves seeming to wink as they shifted this way and that. Point Prospect loomed in the distance, dark rocks crowding around the bottom of it and climbing up to a grassy knoll fenced off with a lookout on top. A family moved about the grassed area, children climbing onto park benches and standing on tiptoe to peer through sturdy lookout binoculars.

"What do you think about the whole situation with Betsy and Frank?" she asked.

Bradford came closer and sat beside her. She leaned her head on his shoulder. "I don't know what to think. Betsy and Frank are institutions on Coral Island. They've been here longer than me, and everyone loves Betsy. I can't imagine she would've done anything wrong. Other than kidnapping her own son, of course, which most people are conflicted over anyway. 'She had her reasons' would be the most obvious response, I suppose."

"That's what I think too. She had to get out of there, and

she was willing to do whatever it took to keep her son safe. I'd do the same thing."

"Me too."

"We can't judge her for that."

"I agree, but you seem to be struggling to come to terms with it. You've brought it up before..."

"I *am* struggling," Charmaine agreed. "I keep going over and over it in my mind. There was something about the way she said it. Anyway, it doesn't matter now. That's the conclusion I'm sticking with. I love Betsy—she's my friend and my boss. She's like family to me since I don't have anyone now but Auntie Finn, her husband and kids, who I haven't even met yet. Sean is gone, and even though I don't ever want to see him again, I miss him. Is that odd?"

"It's how things are with family." Bradford kissed her forehead. "It's complicated. You love them, but sometimes you also can't stand them. You want to be around them, and then when you are, they drive you crazy."

She laughed. "Exactly."

They sat in silence for a few moments.

"How's Evie going in the new office?" Charmaine asked.

Bradford inhaled a deep breath. "She's going great, but there've been a few hiccups with our rental contract and so on. The council is breathing down our necks about an approval we missed, things like that. I'm glad the construction work is finished and Evie can finally take on customers. I know she's excited to stop commuting to Airlie Beach now that she has an office on the island."

"She seemed nervous about it when I spoke to her."

"She'll be fine," Bradford responded. "She's a natural with our customers." He stood to his feet and stretched his arms over his head. "Are you hungry?"

"I could eat," Charmaine replied, standing with him.

"Great. I've got prawns and olives, crackers and cheese in

the galley. It's the usual fare we serve when we take this boat out full of tourists. I'll put it on a plate and be right back." He walked across the boat carefully, ducking beneath a thick, heavy pole attached to a sail.

"I'll join you," Charmaine said.

"This is the spinnaker pole," Bradford said. "Make sure you're careful. It does move about. You should sit and enjoy the view, relax."

"Okay," she replied, with a laugh. "But, I can't sit up here while you're doing all the work."

"Yes, you can," he replied with a wink. "I won't be long. Enjoy yourself."

She sat, took off her hat since it was threatening to fly off at any moment. Then she wrapped her arms around her bent knees. The wind had picked up, and it whipped her hair so she couldn't see very well. Her purse was inside, and there was a brush with a hairband wound around the handle. She should put her hair up and grab a cap, since the straw hat was never going to stay on her head in this wind.

She clambered across the deck. It had begun to sway. She looked up to see dark clouds hustling across the sky from the horizon. She hadn't seen them coming. It looked like it might storm, and soon. Her hair blew against her face, blocking her view completely, and she bent low to move towards the cabin. Just then, something hard and heavy hit her in the back of the head.

With a cry, she fell to her knees. The boat rocked to one side, and she slid down the deck towards the ocean. The water was darker now and surged, slapping against the side of the boat.

With a hand pressed to the back of her throbbing head, she screamed, "Brad!"

Two strong arms wrapped around her body and dragged her to her feet. She squeezed him tight, not wanting to let go.

He led her down into the cabin. Immediately, the wind eased up and she could see again. Her head ached.

"The spinny thing hit me in the head."

"The spinnaker pole?" he asked, leading her to a soft couch.

"Yes, that's it. Ouch."

"I told you to watch out for it."

"I couldn't see — my hair."

He laughed, knelt in front of her, and looked at her hair. "Maybe you should wear it back when we go sailing."

"I will definitely do that next time. Ow!"

He gingerly touched the place where she'd been hit. "There's a knot forming. I'll get you some ice."

When he returned with the ice pack, Charmaine was already feeling better. Although her head still pounded and a headache was beginning to crawl its way across her scalp, she felt warm and safe inside the cabin. Especially with Bradford so close by. He always made her feel safe, something she wasn't used to. She'd been anxious, alone, and afraid for so long that safety and security were foreign concepts to her. But now that she had them, she didn't ever want to let them go.

* * *

After the pill she took helped ease her headache, Charmaine and Bradford emerged from the yacht's cabin to see that the storm had passed by without much more than a few fat drops of rain. The sun shone again and was hotter than it had been before.

"Let's go for a swim," Charmaine suggested, tugging off her soft cotton cover-up.

She dove into the ocean, enjoying the cooling effect of the water on her head and over the small lump where she'd been hurt. She kicked to the surface and drew a deep breath as she shoved her wet hair back from her face and blinked in the dazzling sunshine.

Bradford leapt into the water beside her, tucking his legs up beneath his chin and holding them tight to his chest with both hands. There was an enormous splash where he landed, and the ocean blasted against Charmaine's face. She blinked and wiped her face clear of salt water.

"Thanks for that," she said when his head bobbed to the surface.

He shook his hair with a grin. "No worries." He swam to her with a few easy loping strokes and then slipped his arms around her.

She nestled against his chest. "I wish things could always be like this."

"They can," he whispered, kissing the top of her head.

"I don't know..."

"We make our own future." He stroked her cheek.

"Sometimes life has a tendency to knock us down, even if we're doing everything right." She sighed.

"Are you referring to something specific? Because I know what you mean, with everything that happened to my mother and how her death impacted me, but you haven't spoken about your past. I'd like to know more."

She resisted the urge to pull free from his grasp. Talking about herself, her family, or her past always made her want to run. But Bradford was different. She finally had someone in her life that she trusted completely, and she should let him in. She knew that, but doing it was harder than understanding it. They both climbed the ladder to lie out on the deck side by side. She was puffing lightly when their conversation resumed.

"I told you about the aunt I found on the island."

"Auntie Finn?" he asked.

"Yes, that's right. We lost touch with her because my

mother saw something when she lived here on Coral Island with me and my brother and needed to leave."

"Saw something?"

"She was a kid being babysat by a friend, Mary Brown, when Mary was killed."

Bradford sat up and tented a hand over his eyes to look down at her. "She was there?"

"She witnessed the murder, but the police never believed her description of the assailant because she was so young. So, when she got older, she did some investigating herself and discovered the truth."

"What truth?"

"I don't know for certain. Finn believes she found out the identity of the killer and gathered evidence against them. But whatever it was, it was enough for her to receive death threats. She changed her name, moved away, and never came back. She lost touch with her family and friends. Sean and I never knew the life she should've had."

He blinked. "Wow, that's incredible. I had no idea. Finn told you all this?"

She nodded. "I knew Mum was hiding something. She would start to tell us things, then change the subject. We could never see our grandparents—not after we got a little older, anyway. They called sometimes when I was young, but even the phone calls stopped after a while. I didn't know what was going on, but it seems as though she was terrified to have any connection to Coral Island."

"Did you talk to the police about this?"

"No. According to Finn, Mum believed the police were no help. She spoke to them several times herself, and it never went anywhere other than for her to be run out of town. It seemed to make her even more vulnerable."

Bradford ran his fingers through his hair. "Did she tell anyone who it was?"

"Not that I know of. She might've told Auntie Finn, but Finn acts as though she doesn't know. And maybe she doesn't."

Bradford sat in silence for a few moments, staring out to sea. "The same thing killed my mother. She was unwell, obviously, to do that to herself, but Dad said she was obsessed with finding out the truth. She became a pariah here on the island because so many people sided with Buck and Betsy. Dad says taking sides tore the island apart, but eventually everyone calmed down and life went on. Of course, Bea, Dad and I never recovered."

Charmaine slipped her hand into his and linked their fingers together. "I'm sorry about your mum."

"Thanks. It was a long time ago."

"This one crime impacted so many people's lives. I want to find out the truth about what happened."

He sighed. "Please don't..."

"I won't let it change me. I promise."

He looked at her, desperation in his eyes. "It's already hurt so many of us."

She pressed her lips together. Couldn't he see how much she needed to resolve this? For herself and for her family. For the mother who'd given up everything to keep her safe. For the brother who'd become a lost cause. For the aunt who still worried every night when she locked her house that someone might pay them a visit. Even for him, and the traumatised teen he'd been. "Fine. I'll let it go."

"Thank you," he said with relief tingeing his voice. "Let the police deal with it."

"But I think Betsy knows something. And what was she doing in that cave? Where did the diamond come from?"

His nostrils flared, his eyes full of worry. "You're not letting it go, are you?"

"I'll try." And she meant it.

Six

IT SHOULD RAIN *on a day like this.*

Taya stepped from the back of the black stretch limousine, her red-painted toenails partially hidden in her black peep-toe pumps. The ground was soggy from the previous night, but above her, the sky was cloudless and brilliantly blue.

"Wait, Mum. Let me help you," she said before hurrying around to the other side of the vehicle.

The driver made it to the door before she did and opened it. Her mother climbed out out, and Taya took her arm. Mum leaned heavily on Taya as she walked to the church steps.

"I hope people show up. Your father deserved for people to show up," Mum said with a lump in her throat.

Taya nodded, unable to respond. She didn't care if no one showed up. All she cared about was her mother and her daughter. Now that Dad was gone, she had the two of them to take care of. Her circle was shrinking once again.

"Where's Camden?" Mum asked for the fourth time.

Was her memory going? Or perhaps it was the grief. Taya had answered the question three times already on the drive over.

"She's right behind us, Mum. She wanted to come in her own car with her boyfriend."

"Oh, that's right. She has a boyfriend. I hope he's good to our Camden."

Taya's daughter was twenty-two years old. She'd finished training as a chef in Townsville and had landed a job at one of the best resorts in the area, where she'd met her boyfriend. He was the restaurant manager, and the two of them had spent six months getting to know each other before meeting each other's families. Camden was sensible and liked to take things slow, something Taya admired in her strong-willed child.

She turned to look back over her shoulder as Camden's blue hatchback pulled into the parking lot. She stopped to wait, Mum standing with her, while Camden and Michael climbed out of the car and walked hand in hand to the church.

Camden kissed her grandmother's cheek, her eyes red-rimmed. Then she embraced Taya. Taya held on to her daughter for several long seconds, fighting the urge to burst into tears. Then she took a deep breath and pulled back.

Camden offered a wobbly smile. "You okay, Mum?"

"I'm surviving. I don't know how to face each day without him." Her voice broke. "We were going to retire," she said quietly as tears pooled in her eyes. "We never got the chance."

Taya bent to hug her mother. Mum was a tiny woman—buxom, but short. Taya had inherited her father's height, as had Camden. They'd also both taken after her father with their shiny dark hair and brown eyes, whereas Mum had grey eyes and, when she was younger, wavy dark blonde hair. Now it was grey, like her eyes, but the waves were still there.

"Let's go inside," Taya said. "People will be arriving soon, and we need to greet them."

"I don't know how we're supposed to do that," Camden muttered as they walked into the church together. "We're the ones who are grieving. Why should we have to arrange the funeral and then make everyone else feel better?"

Taya bit down on her lower lip. She didn't have any answers for her child other than that's how things were done.

"I'm sorry, Mum. I'm not complaining for myself. I know how much you've had to do to get this whole thing arranged, and it seems wrong that it's on your shoulders when you're going through something so hard."

Taya patted her arm as they took their seats at the front of the chapel. "It's okay, sweetie. I don't know why it is the way it is, but who else should do it? There's no one else. Only us. And yes, it's hard, but it's probably a good way to say goodbye as well."

If she hadn't been required to take care of the funeral arrangements, Taya would've simply disappeared into her bedroom, curled up on the bed, and not emerged for days. She would've cried into her pillow, eaten too much chocolate, and watched sappy movies. Instead, she'd looked through photographs and videos of Dad to add to a reel or to print out for the service, she'd picked out his favourite songs to play, hired a string quartet, located the pastor her dad had loved and who had since retired, and arranged for family to fly in and stay at the inn. There were a million things she'd managed in the past two weeks since her father died, and every step had brought her to a place of frustration and grief, and then resignation and acceptance.

It was all part of the healing process, she supposed. Even if it did seem like cruel and unusual punishment.

The funeral itself went quickly. Taya stood up to give the eulogy and managed to get through it without crying. Evie, Bea, and Charmaine sat near the middle of the chapel and smiled at her encouragingly. The entire chapel was packed with people. So many of the residents had come out to pay respects to her father, the man who'd built an empire from his home in the tiny hamlet of Blue Shoal on Coral Island. He'd never given up the place to move to the big city, and people appreciated that about him. He'd called Blue Shoal his home for most of his life, as had Taya. Her family was familiar with almost every single resident on the island. They'd employed a lot of them over the years—had been to BBQs with them or attended school with them.

There were also many businesspeople in attendance from across the world. Some of the top employees and resort managers from throughout the resort network had flown in to attend the funeral, and there were dark suits and red-rimmed eyes everywhere she looked. It brought a lump to her throat when she stood at the front to deliver the eulogy, as she spoke about her father—the man he was, the parent he'd been to her, and his achievements. She talked about how much he'd loved her mother and the community where he'd spent his life.

Finally, it was over. She spoke with as many of those in attendance as she could before leaving with her mother in the limousine. Camden and Michael followed in their car. They travelled back to the house, where caterers had taken over the kitchen and wait staff were scurrying through the living areas setting up tables with tablecloths, candles, a condolences book, and drink stations for the wake.

Taya looked around for Andrew and saw him parking his car in front of the garage. He'd avoided the valets who stood in the circular driveway waiting to park guests' cars on the road outside the estate. She waved him over and stood on tiptoe to embrace him with a deep exhale. It was good to be in his arms again, and she felt sudden fatigue wash over her.

"I'm glad you're here."

He squeezed her. "Your eulogy was perfect."

"Thank you. And I'm sorry I ran out on you the other day. I was in a panic. I should've driven with you, but I couldn't think clearly."

"It's fine. I understand completely," he replied. "When my wife died, I could barely function at all. So, I think you're doing well, considering."

She'd always meant to ask him more about his wife's death, but hadn't found the opportunity. It seemed like a sensitive topic and she didn't want to be insensitive, but she was curious.

"I don't mean to pry, but you mentioned that she was killed..."

"By religious extremists."

"I'm so sorry. That must've been devastating for you."

"It was," he said, his eyes clouding over. "But enough about that. What can I do to help?"

"I think everything's been taken care of. Come inside with me, and we'll find a drink. At some stage, we need to talk about the business and what Dad's sudden death will mean."

Andrew linked his fingers through hers and then kissed the back of her hand. They stepped into the house and walked through the cavernous halls, her heels tapping on the polished tiles. They found her mother, Camden, and Michael in the kitchen. Mum was pouring Tom Collins cocktails into several tall glasses. The icy drink looked delicious and exactly what Taya needed. She'd barely had a thing to drink all day, and her mouth salivated at the sight of the cold liquid.

"Thank you," she said as Mum handed her one. "You should sit down, Mum. You don't have to serve anyone— we've hired staff exactly for that reason."

"I don't mind. I'm not sure what to do with myself if I don't keep busy," Mum explained with trembling lips.

"Then do whatever it is you prefer, Grandma," Camden said, coming around the bench to embrace her.

Taya's heart swelled with pride over the loving, thoughtful daughter she'd somehow managed to raise on her own while running a very demanding boutique inn. How had she managed it? She'd purposely avoided asking her parents for help much of the time, since she was adamant about doing it on her own and not needing to rely on the family fortune or name. Now she realized how ridiculous that had been — what was family for if not to help each other during the hard times? And they had helped her, just not as often or as much as they would've liked, Taya was sure. They'd told her often enough they wanted to do more. Still, Camden had grown into a wonderful, hardworking, strong and independent woman despite Taya's stubbornness.

Taya patted Camden on the back. "Thank you, sweetheart. Grandpa would be so proud of you."

Camden faced her, eyes glistening. "Do you think so?"

"He told me all the time how much he loved you and how wonderful you are. He was proud that you decided to become a chef — he'd always said that chefs are the hardest-working members of the Paradise Resorts family. I think he hoped that one day you'd work for him."

Camden wiped her eyes. "I hoped that too. What will happen to the company now?"

Taya's heart skipped a beat. It was a question she didn't have an answer for. "I suppose it will be okay. Dad set it up to thrive without him." Her words weren't convincing. He was the heart of the business. How would it work without him?

"Your mother will take over, of course," her mother said. "That's what Grandpa wanted."

"Is that true, Mum?" Camden blinked big doe-like brown eyes.

Taya swallowed. "Yes, he wanted me to take over. But I'm not ready yet, and I don't know how the board will respond. There's still a lot to think about and get through before we're at that point."

"The board knows what your father's wishes were. He spoke to them about it and put it into writing. They won't be a problem," her mother assured her as she wiped down the spotless bench top with a wet cloth.

Was it true? Taya had presumed the board would have their own thoughts about who should run Paradise Resorts after her father's death. They knew how green she was, that she'd barely had time to get to know the business. She'd only been there a little over a year—it wasn't long enough. She couldn't fill his shoes.

Seven

"UNO!" Harry called, laying down his hand of cards on the coffee table. He, Dani and Damien had flown to Coral Island for the weekend, even though it'd only been a month since their last visit. Dani said she wanted Bea to get to know Damien better. Bea grudgingly accepted that getting to know the professor allowed her to see her children more often.

Bea stared at the cards splayed out between her fingers, then grimaced.

Dani groaned. "No, not again. He's won four games in a row. Mum..."

"What? It's not my fault. I have three useless cards. I thought you'd at least have a Draw 4 card."

"I told you I had nothing."

Damien raised a hand to his forehead. "Do we have to argue about it? I'm getting a headache."

Bea stifled a smile. "I'm sorry, Damien. Maybe we should take a break. I'll make coffee and slice some of that cinnamon tea cake I made earlier."

"I'll help," Harry said with a meaningful glance at his sister.

Dani paid no attention and lay back on the rug that took up most of the living room floor. "Harry's a cheater!"

Harry laughed. "I never cheat. You're terrible at card games."

He followed Bea into the kitchen and pulled the cake tin close before searching for a knife. "You okay, Mum?"

"I'm fine," Bea said, although she seemed to be experiencing the same headache as Damien. "A bit of a headache. It's nothing."

"Maybe you're both coming down with something."

"I don't think so. I'm..." She bit down on her tongue. No need to say something snippy she'd regret.

"It's okay, Mum. It's only me. You can say it."

"I'm still getting used to having Damien around. That's all."

He grinned. "He's such a—"

"Harry," she warned him. "Let's be kind."

"Mum, you want to call him names. Let's say the things we want to say, and we'll both feel much better."

She laughed, slapping Harry's shoulder gently. "You're a bad influence. Did I ever tell you that?"

The phone rang, and Bea slipped it between her chin and shoulder so she could talk while she added coffee to the espresso machine.

"Hi, Dad," she trilled. "Are you on your way? We're having Mexican food tonight. I know you're not a huge fan, so I've set aside some salmon for you to eat with your salad instead if you'd prefer it."

Her father's voice rasped down the line. "Don't panic, Bea. Everything's okay."

Her heart dropped and she set down the bag of coffee on the bench. "What? Why?"

"I'm fine, but I've had an accident."

"What happened? Where are you?"

"I was spearfishing with Betsy, and I ran into a little reef shark. He had a nibble on my leg—mostly curious, I think. Nothing disastrous. The ambulance is on its way, and Betsy's taking care of me. I thought you might like a phone call."

Beatrice hurried into the living room and waved frantically at Aidan. "I'm on my way. Where are you?"

"I'm at the cove below the house."

"I'll be there as soon as I can make it."

"You should probably head to the hospital instead, and I'll meet you there."

"Okay. I'll see you at the hospital, Dad."

By the time she'd finished the conversation and hung up the phone, Aidan stood beside her, hands on his hips. The others stared in shock.

"What's happened to Pa?" Dani asked, wide-eyed.

"Shark bite, but he says he's okay. I'm going to the hospital. I'm sorry about dinner, everyone." She turned to the right, then to the left, then spun in a circle. What was she doing? She needed something.

"Your purse?" Aidan asked.

She nodded. "Yes, and keys."

"I'll drive," he replied. "You're too upset."

"Okay. Thanks."

"I'm coming too." Harry stepped out of the kitchen and raised a hand. "I'm not staying here."

"Me too," Dani added.

"I'll stay and get the tacos ready. I'm sure he'll be fine," Damien offered.

"Thank you, Damien. I appreciate that," Beatrice said as Aidan slipped her purse over her shoulder. "Let's go, then."

* * *

The drive to the Coral Island hospital wasn't a long one, but it seemed interminable. When Aidan parked the car outside the small redbrick building, Bea leapt out and hurried towards the doors of the emergency room, purse held close to her side.

"Wait, Mum!" Dani shouted behind her.

Aidan, Harry and Dani all jogged to catch up with her, and the four of them bustled through the emergency room to a desk behind glass windows where a woman in scrubs sat staring at a screen.

"I'm looking for Elias Rushton," Bea said through the square opening.

The woman ran her finger down the screen and tapped it once. "He's being seen by the doctor. I'll go and check on him for you. Are you family?"

"Yes," Harry replied.

Bea looked at her son. His face was drawn and pale. She shouldn't have worried her family so much—Dad had told her he was fine. But then, he often downplayed when things went wrong so she wouldn't be disturbed. She couldn't help feeling anxious until she knew for certain that he was all right.

"It's going to be okay, honey," she said, rubbing Harry's arm.

She turned to Dani, offering her a wan smile. "Pa is strong. I'm sure he's fine."

Aidan looped an arm around her shoulders. "You should tell that to your face."

She shook her head. "That bad?"

"You gave us all a fright," Aidan said.

"But what if..?" Her unfinished question hung in the air between them.

"Let's wait to see how he is before we jump to conclusions," Aidan replied.

They waited in a row of plastic chairs against one wall of the ER for another hour. A nurse came to tell them Dad was having surgery. Harry and Dani played on their phones. Bea paced, then sat and stared at the wall, then paced again. Aidan made phone calls about his real estate development project, talking at loud volumes outside the hospital and glancing through the automatic glass doors every now and then to check that they were still there.

Finally, a nurse came walking towards them. "Rushton family?"

Bea stood and ran both sweaty palms down the front of her shorts. "Yes, that's us."

"The surgery went well. Elias had some tissue damage in his left thigh and calf, but he's going to be fine."

Bea exhaled a long, slow breath. "Thank you so much."

The nurse looked tired. "He's in recovery. You can see him if you like. He's still sleeping, but I'm sure he'd like to see you when he wakes."

"That would be great," Harry said.

Bea waved Aidan inside. He quickly hung up the phone and hurried to join them, then they all followed the nurse through various doors and down hallways until they reached a large room filled with medical instruments. Dad lay on a bed, his eyes shut. A sheet was pulled up over his body. He looked like he was sleeping.

Tears sprang to Bea's eyes. "Dad," she whispered, moving forward to take his hand in hers.

Dani went to the other side of the bed to hold his hand as well. Harry watched quietly, blinking rapidly.

The nurse checked a few items on the clipboard. Then she took his pulse and ran some quiet tests. After a while, his eyes fluttered open. He made a sound.

"Dad, you're awake," Bea said, wiping her cheeks dry.

His gaze went from her face, to Harry's, then Dani's and finally Aidan's. "Why the long faces?"

They laughed and cried together, chattering about

nothing much. Dad was still loopy from the anaesthetic, so for the next half an hour he didn't seem to know anything about why he was there or what had happened. Finally, the others went to the cafeteria to get something to eat and drink. Bea stayed behind while Dad dozed.

His eyes blinked open again. "You still here?"

"I'm not going anywhere, Dad. You feeling okay? Can I get you something?"

He nodded. "Thirsty."

She reached for the cup of cold water they'd filled for him earlier and set it to his lips for him to drink.

"I'm not an invalid, you know. I can get my own water."

"You've had an accident, Dad. And right now, you are a bit of an invalid. I know how frustrating that is for you to admit." She laughed softly. "Drink up. You're going to be fine."

"It was a shark, wasn't it?" he asked.

It was the first time he'd said anything about his accident that made any sense. "Yes, that's right. Do you remember it?"

"Of course I do. I'm not going to forget something like that. It came out of nowhere. I was spearfishing up against the reef when there it was—chomping down on my leg like I was a lamb roast."

He was impossible. How many times had she told him not to go spearfishing? Let alone at dusk. "Dad…"

"I know, I should stop the spearfishing. Only Betsy wanted to go, and I thought it might be fun."

"What's the deal with the two of you?" She'd never discussed this with her dad before, but from the moment she'd first met Betsy, she'd noticed some kind of tension between the older lady and her father. Betsy had insinuated several times that they were close, but Bea had no idea how close.

"What do you mean?"

"Are you dating? Friends? Neighbours? What kind of relationship do you have?"

Dad's eyes narrowed. "When did we swap roles? You sound like you're my father, not the other way around."

He was right. She was acting like a concerned parent. "Sorry—it's none of my business. I'm only curious."

He grunted. "We're friends."

"Nothing more?"

"We spend time together and enjoy each other's company. No, it's not romantic, if that's what you're inferring. We both like to fish and we're around the same age. She's a little older than me, but she's a nice lady and we don't have to pretend to be someone else. We like to sit quietly and fish or talk about politics. Nothing too deep. It's nice to have friends."

Suddenly she felt ashamed of prying. "You're right, Dad. It is nice to have friends. I'm glad you have Betsy in your life. My only concern is that she might not be the person you think she is."

"Who is she, then?"

"It's possible she had another name when she lived in the USA. She might be on the run from the law. The girls and I have been doing a bit of research. We think she's a fugitive, and she's hiding out on the island."

Dad laughed. "You've been watching too much *CSI*."

"I'm serious, Dad."

He laughed harder until he coughed. "Stop, honey—that's silly."

Bea shook her head. "Fine. Don't believe me. By the way, where is she?"

"She fainted."

"What?" Bea hadn't expected that. "Is she okay?"

"I don't know. She came with me in the ambulance. She got light headed, so they wheeled her off somewhere else."

"I'll go and check on her." Bea stood to her feet.

Dani, Harry and Aidan returned at that moment, drinks in hand plus a takeaway bag, which Aidan handed to Bea. "I got you some nuggets. There wasn't much."

"That's fine—thanks. I'm going to look for Betsy. She came in with Dad and then fainted. I want to make sure she's okay."

Aidan's brow furrowed. "I hope she isn't hurt."

"I don't know, but I'll find out."

Bea headed back to the reception area, where she asked about Betsy. She was told the older lady's son had picked her up and taken her home, that she was fine and had simply been lightheaded from too much sunshine and not enough hydration.

Bea took a seat in the waiting area and laid her head back against the wall. The adrenaline that'd pumped through her veins for hours had now abated. All she felt was tired. Her phone rang, and she pressed it to her ear, eyes still shut.

"Hello?"

"Hey, Bea. It's Penny."

She straightened in her seat, a smile forming on her lips. "Penny, how are you? It's so nice to hear your voice."

"I'm great. Listen, Bea, we're coming back to the island for the reunion. I told Rowan we can't miss it, even though he's not so thrilled about the idea. But I desperately want to see all of you."

"I'm glad. It's not going to be a big deal or anything, but I think it will be nice. It wouldn't be the same without you and Rowan there."

Penny inhaled a slow breath. "Also, I have something to tell you."

"Oh?"

"I'm pregnant."

Eight

AS CHARMAINE STOOD outside the front door of the blue house with the climbing vines hanging haphazardly from a swinging potted plant, she drew a deep breath. Then she raised her fist to knock on the door. Its peeled paint didn't match the blue of the house, instead in a random aqua tone, but it worked in a quaint beach house kind of way.

When the door swung open, a child of about twelve stared out at her from beneath too-long hair that hung in her eyes, or *his* eyes. She couldn't tell.

"I'm Chaz," she said.

The child nodded mutely, then swung the screen door open.

Charmaine stepped inside and was greeted with a cacophony of noises and smells. The kitchen was at the back of the house, and she followed the child through a messy living room piled with musical instruments, half-read books, and dog chew toys.

Finn stood at a stove, dressed in a pair of shorts, a T-shirt, and a large apron. Her short hair was mussed. "Chaz, you made it. Grab a seat. I'll get you something to drink." She waved a wooden spoon as she spoke, and flecks of something spattered around her.

Charmaine pulled a stool from the edge of the bench and sat, unsure how to act in a place of so much bedlam. She wasn't accustomed to it—she'd grown up with a mother who liked things orderly, minimal, and neat, and a brother who barely emerged from his bedroom.

Several teenagers lounged around the living room, one leg hanging over the side of an armchair or two feet protruding from the end of a couch, screens or books pressed close to their faces.

"What would you like to drink?" Finn stirred something in a pan on the stove.

"Anything is fine."

"I have a chardonnay open."

"Perfect," Charmaine replied.

Finn moved to the refrigerator and pulled out a bottle. She poured wine into two glasses. "Ed is running a little late, but he'll be home any minute. He was on the mainland today fixing some pipes at the water purification plant."

"Wow. That sounds like a responsible job."

She laughed. "Very. I'm the irresponsible one in the family. And I'll introduce you to the kids at dinner. There's no point trying to drag them away from their devices right now. And besides, I want to talk to you without them listening in for a few minutes." She lowered her voice and offered Charmaine a wink.

Charmaine smoothed her wrinkled floral print dress. She'd cycled into town in the gathering dark, the first time she'd attempted that. She'd purchased a bike lamp to help her see better and to be seen better. And it'd worked well, apart from all the insects she'd inhaled. She ran her tongue over her teeth to check none of them were still there.

"I didn't bring Watson. I thought he might leap out of the

basket on my bike and disappear into the bush never to be seen again." The last thing she wanted to do was end up spending her night traipsing through the unlit bushland on her own looking for her cat.

"Oh, dear. I forgot you don't have a car. I should've collected you."

"It's fine. I like riding."

"Maybe Ed can drive you home after dinner."

"Thanks! That would be nice."

She took the wine Finn offered, and the two of them clinked their glasses together. Charmaine was overwhelmed by a wave of emotion for a moment. She was standing in a warm, welcoming kitchen, surrounded by family. Granted, she hadn't met the children yet, but she was their cousin. She'd never had cousins before—none that she knew of, anyway.

They each drank, then Finn switched off the stove and came around the bench. "Let's sit outside where it's cool and away from prying eyes."

They went through a doorway to a back deck, and each took a seat in a comfortable wicker chair. The chairs faced a dark backyard. Charmaine couldn't see much, but it looked to be a similar style to the inside of the house — plenty of plants, shrubs, flowers and bushes all muddled together in a messy, artistic, beautiful garden.

"I love your house. It's very *you*," Charmaine said, taking another sip of wine.

"Thank you. I'll show you some of my artwork later. But for now, I wanted to talk to you about something."

"I'm listening," Chaz replied, her curiosity piqued.

"I didn't tell you everything the last time we spoke."

"That's okay. You don't have to."

"Yes, I do." Finn hesitated. "I don't know where to start. So, I guess I'll jump right in."

"That's probably a good approach."

57

Finn inhaled a slow breath, then began. "Your mother was always a troublemaker."

"That sounds about right."

Finn laughed. "I don't mean in the sense that she was a criminal or anything like that. But if someone didn't tell the whole truth, she would poke and prod them until they gave in and confessed. If there was a mystery, she'd get to the bottom of it. She didn't much seem to care who was hurt or inconvenienced in the process. She only wanted to know everything. I think that more than anything, she was a curious person."

"It's hard to think of her that way. She didn't seem particularly curious to me."

"By the time you were old enough to notice, she'd changed her ways. It'd brought her nothing but trouble, so she'd learned to keep her curiosity quiet."

"You told me she witnessed Mary Brown's murder."

"Yes. Mary was babysitting her, and they were playing hide-and-seek. When Helen was hiding in a closet, she saw Mary killed."

"Did she ever tell you who she saw?" That wasn't something Finn had mentioned, and Charmaine hadn't pursued it earlier. But clearly, she wanted to get something off her chest, and Charmaine was desperate to know the truth.

Finn nodded slowly. Charmaine gasped. "Who was it?"

"Well, she didn't exactly tell me who it was, only clues to finding out their identity. I'm not sure I should tell you what I know. The knowledge has cost my family a lot. I don't want you to have to carry that burden."

"Okay." Frustration itched along her spine. She should know the truth. It was her mother's secret, and she'd taken it to her grave. Keeping that secret now benefited no one.

"I mentioned that she found something the last time we spoke. The thing that she found — it was jewellery. I saw it, she showed me a necklace, a bracelet, and a ring. The necklace and bracelet had diamonds, but the ring didn't have a jewel in it—looked like it'd fallen out. Also, they were kind of dirty and old-looking, so I didn't understand how valuable they were when I saw them. But Helen told me she thought they would be worth a lot."

Charmaine's heart thundered in her chest. Did Finn know that she had the jewellery? Did she suspect? Charmaine wasn't sure who she could trust. The promise of easy money changed people. "Did she get the pieces valued?"

Finn's eyes were bright. "No, she didn't want to tip anyone off that she'd found them. Something like that, worth so much money—it's got to have people looking for it."

"You're probably right." The only person Charmaine had been worried about was Sean. But perhaps there was someone else looking for the jewellery, someone who suspected she had it. If they discovered she was Helen's daughter, her life could be in danger like her mother's had been. "It's a shame. We'll never know if it was valuable or fake."

"Helen said she found it in a box hidden under the sand in a cave. I wasn't sure if she made that part up to protect herself. Maybe she stole the jewellery from someone and didn't want me to know. But whatever the truth was, she was scared. That part I'm certain of."

Sweat trickled down Charmaine's back, and her head pounded. Her mother had found the jewellery hidden in a cave. It had to have been the same cave where they'd followed Betsy that day and found the loose diamond in the sand. What had Betsy been there to find? Did she find what she was looking for? And how had the diamond ended up where it was?

"That was when the harassment started. Whoever had owned the jewellery knew she had it, or at least suspected it. She was spooked and left town. But they continued harassing us, breaking into our house and tossing the place for years afterwards. Just when we thought it was over, they'd do it all over again. It drove Mum and Dad crazy. I feel terrible when I think about what they went through — as well as losing their daughter that way."

Charmaine stood to her feet. "Do you mind if I freshen up in the bathroom?"

"Of course, honey. It's down the hall to your left. I think I hear Ed's car in the drive. Dinner's ready, so wash up and we'll eat."

* * *

After dinner, Charmaine slowly pedalled her bike back home in the dark. She'd politely declined Ed's offer to drive her home. After a lovely dinner of roast pork, crispy potatoes, and freshly roasted vegetables, she was stuffed full of food and feeling much better about everything.

Ed and Finn had four children — the twelve-year-old who'd turned out to be a girl, plus three teenagers, two boys and another girl. All of them were lovely, polite children who showed a quiet interest in their new cousin. They'd chatted her ear off after a while, the reserved façade gone in short order when they discovered she was as proficient at gaming as they were. She'd spent enough hours playing against her brother over the years. At least the effort had been good for something.

What she wanted now was some time with her thoughts, and the bike ride home gave her that. She didn't feel spooked riding on her own along the road late at night. She left her bike lamp off to allow her eyes to adjust to the darkness, and the moon shone bright overhead, lighting her way. There were no cars at this time of night, and her bike was virtually silent as she cruised down the narrow, winding road.

An owl hooted in the distance. Stars twinkled in a blanket of light above her head. She'd never get over how beautiful the night sky was on Coral Island. There was very little light pollution, and the number of visible stars were many times more than there had been in the city.

The only sounds were the hush of waves lapping gently at the nearby shore and the fossicking of nocturnal animals and birds as they went about their nightly search for food. She loved Coral Island. She loved the birds, the animals, the ocean, the sky—everything about it felt like home. It'd become a part of her soul in such a short space of time. She couldn't imagine ever leaving.

But what if her life was in danger? What if Finn talked to someone, to the wrong person, and let it slip who Charmaine was—that she was a Hilton, and Helen Hilton's heir? They might figure out she'd inherited the jewellery, and if it was worth as much as she thought it might be, she could very well be in trouble.

She rolled her bike down the track to the cottage, then jumped off and set the bike against the wall. Inside, Watson greeted her with an arched back and a lazy yawn.

"How'd you go, boy? Miss me? Sorry I don't have any leftovers for you tonight, but I can probably find you a can of cat food if you're hungry."

The cat followed her to the pantry, and she opened a can into his bowl. Her back slid down the cabinet, and she sat on the floor beside Watson and stroked him as he ate. His body rose to meet her hand.

"What am I going to do about those jewels? They're safe for now, but maybe I'm not." She crossed her arms over her chest, her thoughts jumbled and pained over the idea of leaving Coral Island behind forever to keep herself safe as her mother had done before her.

There was a sound outside on the front porch. Something clattered. Then there was silence. Charmaine's heart jumped into her throat, pounding.

What was that? Maybe it was the killer, come to get the jewellery that was safely stowed in the bank vault in Kellyville.

Heart still pounding, she crawled on hands and knees to the front door. Then there was a great bang, and something shattered. She leaned her back against the door. Adrenaline pumped through her veins. Perhaps she should make a run for it. She reached up and turned the lock in the doorknob by her head. Then she slowly inched her way up the door to peer through the base of the windowpane.

With bated breath, she peered to the left, then to the right. Her bike lay on its side on the front porch. There was an over-turned potted plant nearby in pieces. And right beside it, a possum stood on its four legs, peering directly at her.

Laughing with relief, she straightened her back and pressed both hands to her chest, willing her thundering heart to return to its normal rhythm. Then she flicked off the porch light and headed for bed. She'd had enough excitement for one night.

Nine

TAYA STARED at the cursor on her computer screen. She blinked. The cursor blinked. What should she write? She needed to draft a companywide email to communicate with the staff about her father's passing and what it would mean for the group, but she couldn't find the words. There had been an announcement the day after his passing but she wanted to draft something more heartfelt now that the funeral was over. How should she describe a man who formed a company out of nothing and built it to be one of the country's most successful resort chains in history? A man who knew most of the employees by name and cared about their lives, who'd given his everything to be their employer, provider, friend?

She blinked again then turned away to cross her arms and stare at her office wall. Already her assistant had asked when they would be moving her to the CEO office down the hall. She didn't have an answer. She didn't want to go in there, let alone set up her workspace there. She missed her father so much, it still hurt in the base of her throat whenever she thought about it. He'd only been gone three weeks. How would she cope with a year, ten years?

LILLY MIRREN

Susan poked her head through the office door. "I'm going to lunch. Can I get you anything before I go?"

Taya shook her head. "I have to write this email. Any ideas?"

"Be yourself. People like genuine warmth, and you have plenty of that."

"Thanks," Taya replied. "Is Andrew in the office yet?"

"I believe he's been at his desk for about half an hour. Do you want me to ask him to meet you?"

"Yes, please. See if he's free for lunch."

"Will do."

Susan pulled the door shut behind her. Within a few moments, the phone rang. It was Susan calling to say that Andrew would stop by her office to take her to lunch. Taya hung up the phone and stared at the blank screen. She typed two words.

Dear employees,

Then she deleted it and chewed on her lower lip. "Employees" was too impersonal. She should use a more congenial term, like "fellow workers" or "staff." Fellow workers? She wasn't writing a communist manifesto. She groaned and pressed both hands to her face. This was impossible. The thing she dreaded most was that she was bound to burst into tears halfway through the email, and she'd cried so many tears in recent days, she was exhausted. She didn't have the energy or the fluid reserves for more.

There was a tap at the door, and she called, "Come in."

Andrew walked in with a smile on his face. His dark brown eyes glowed, and his black hair fell smoothly on either side of a part. He strode with purpose to her desk, took her hand, and pulled her up into his arms. She fell against his chest with her eyes pressed shut. It felt good to be held, as though the troubles in her life might fade away for a single moment and she could relax and be at ease.

64

"I'm so glad to see you," she said. "I hope you weren't busy."

"Not too busy to see you." He kissed her.

"I'm trying to write the email to the company, and it's taking me longer than I thought it would. I have so much to get done, I don't know how I'm going to manage it all."

"Is there anything I can help with?" he asked.

She sighed. "Not really. I'm complaining, and you're a good listener. It helps more than you know."

"I'm glad to listen," he replied with another kiss. "Where should we eat today?"

"Let's go to the Blue Shoal Inn. I miss it today more than ever. I need to go there—it feels like I'm closer to Dad. He used to come to the inn every couple of weeks to have lunch. I thought at the time that he was doing it to check on the inn, but now I know he wanted to see me. I'd do the same thing for Camden if I lived closer to her."

"I need to talk to you about something before we go," Andrew said.

Taya leaned against her desk and crossed her arms. "Shoot."

Andrew paced to the wall and back again. It piqued Taya's curiosity — she'd never seen him so unnerved. It must be something serious.

His brow furrowed, and he stopped pacing. "Do you remember our discussion about my wife's death?"

"Of course."

"The same people who killed her are harassing my parents."

"Oh, no. I'm so sorry!"

He shook his head. "They're getting older, and they're afraid. There are death threats, and someone broke into their house. It's escalating."

"I don't understand why anyone would do that."

"It's about religious differences. As you know, we're Hindu, and there is another religious group in the area we're from who take issue with our beliefs. It doesn't make any sense, but it happens more often than you might think. Anyway, I've asked them to move to Australia to live with me, and they're coming next week."

Taya blinked. "Wow, really? That's very sudden."

He shrugged. "We've been planning it for a while."

But he hadn't said anything to her about it. Her stomach did a flip. Why had he kept something so big to himself? They'd been dating for over a year, and yet he kept her at arm's length so much of the time. He rarely opened up about his feelings or what was going on in his life. She had a moment of clarity — when they were together she did most of the talking. How had they gotten this far without her knowing him better?

"Okay, well, I think that's great. They'll feel a lot safer on Coral Island."

"I think so too," he said. "We've already applied for a permanent residency visa, and they've received provisional approval."

"So, you've been working on this for a long time, then?"

"Yes, like I said, a while."

She pressed a smile to her face. "How wonderful."

"The thing is," he began, his gaze firmly on the floor, "my parents are very traditional. And they wouldn't like our relationship."

"Oh." Taya's smile faded. "I see."

"They'll be new to this country, afraid, nervous... They'll take up a lot of my free time. I'd like us to cool things off, until I get everything sorted out. When they're established and they're used to the lifestyle and culture here, maybe we can restart where we left off."

Taya's heart plummeted into her stomach. Cool things off? "You're breaking up with me?"

"Temporarily," he replied, finally meeting her gaze.

"Okay. Thanks for letting me know." She was numb. Her head spun. She sat with a huff.

"Are you okay?"

She nodded. "Fine, fine. I've got to finish this email, though, so I'll talk to you later this afternoon."

"I thought you wanted to grab lunch around noon."

She looked at him, her eyes narrowed. Did he think he could break up with her and then eat a nice lunch together? "Uh, no, not today. Maybe another time. As I said, I have a lot to do."

"Okay, another time. I'll see you later."

Andrew left and Taya spun her chair slowly, not stopping. Around and around she went, staring at her feet. She loved her red peep-toe pumps. They looked good and were comfortable. Besides, they popped next to the charcoal suit she was wearing. People often complimented her on those shoes. She should get more red shoes. Why was she thinking about shoes? She didn't want to think about what had happened. It was too much, after the emotional rollercoaster of the last few weeks.

Why would he break up with her? His parents didn't approve? Unless they didn't know about her. Maybe he was using his poor elderly parents as his excuse to break things off. But why would he do that three weeks after her own father's death? She'd never imagined he could be so heartless. They worked together—now she'd have to avoid him at staff meetings, executive meetings, board meetings... She shuddered. Why hadn't she listened to the little voice inside her head that'd warned against dating at work? This was fast becoming her worst nightmare.

Ten

BEATRICE NEEDED to place an order for the floral arrangements for the reunion dinner. Charmaine had of course offered to put in the order, since she was planning the event and she worked at Betsy's Florals, but Bea wanted to see Betsy. It was time she had a conversation with the older woman.

There were so many questions lurking in her thoughts around Betsy and her past, her connection to Bea's parents, and so much more. But she and her friends had tiptoed around Betsy and Buck, doing research at the library or online instead of simply confronting her with what they knew. It was time to ask some questions.

Bea nudged open the door to the narrow florist shop and glanced around. There was no one inside. A bell jangled above her head, and soon Betsy emerged from the back with a grin on her face.

"Beatrice Rushton. How good to see you."

She shuffled forwards and gave Bea a hug. Bea hadn't expected that. They weren't exactly close. But she returned the embrace anyway, then stepped aside to study a painting on the wall she hadn't seen before. It was an impressionist seascape with splashes of intense colour and a feeling of urgency in the leaping froth of the waves. It drew her in and made her feel emotional, as though it was reaching deep down into her soul. She didn't often experience such a visceral reaction to artwork, and it took her by surprise.

"This is beautiful, Betsy. I don't think I'm familiar with the artist."

"That's one of Chaz's paintings. She's good, isn't she?"

"Chaz did this? Wow. I love it."

Betsy pressed her hands to her hips. "She's got a great eye."

"I think I'll buy this for the house."

"Wonderful choice," Betsy replied, reaching up to take the painting from the wall. "I'll wrap it up for you."

"I have to order some flowers for our high school reunion as well," Bea added. "So, take your time. I'm going to look around a little bit."

Bea strolled around the store, checking out arrangements and flowers. Finally, she decided on an assortment of native plants—wattle, bottlebrush, banksia, waxflower, grevillea. She pointed out the arrangements she preferred to Betsy, who noted them down in a small book with a pencil. She chewed on the end of the pencil, brow furrowed while Bea spoke, then her pencil went flying across the page as she wrote the order.

Finally, they were finished, and Bea followed Betsy to the cash register to pay. "Thank you for all your help. It makes things a lot easier that Chaz works here and can pick them up to bring to the event. She's planning the reunion for us—did I mention that?"

"You didn't mention it," Betsy replied. "But that's positive — she'll go far in this industry if she wants. She's artistic and does detailed work. She's a good girl."

"I think so too," Bea agreed. She'd wanted to bring up the subject of her mother, but it never seemed like the right time.

She had questions. Perhaps Betsy would give her the answers she was looking for. She cleared her throat. "I remember when I first met you. You said something about my mother's death being a waste. That it shouldn't have happened."

Betsy's gaze met hers. Her pupils dilated until her eyes were mostly black against the glow of the shop lights behind her. "That's right. It shouldn't have."

"Did you mean anything by that?"

"Like what?" she asked, her American accent growing stronger by the minute.

"Was there something that could've been done to prevent her taking her own life?"

Betsy sighed. "I think so. But what do I know?"

"By Dad or someone else?"

Betsy's eyes narrowed, and she studied Bea closely. "What are you getting at, darlin'?"

"Did you have something to do with her death?" Bea almost whispered the words, and her heart thudded as they left her lips.

Betsy didn't move a muscle. Then she spoke. "Why do you ask that?"

"I know about the cave, Betsy. I found the box that was stashed there and handed it in to the police."

"I get that, Bea. But what does that have to do with me?" Betsy lowered herself into the chair behind the register, seeming suddenly older than her eighty-plus years. Her face was lined, her eyes red-rimmed with dark shadows beneath them. She must not be sleeping well.

"Chaz and Bradford saw you go into the cave and come out again. What were you doing in there?"

Betsy's lips pulled into a lazy grin. "Aren't y'all the little detectives?"

"We know about your old life in California and that you kidnapped your son and ran from the law."

Betsy's smile faded. "Oh, do you now? Well, I figured, since Chaz had all those clippings."

"Did you kill my mother?"

Betsy grunted. "Of course not. She took her own life—there was nothing suspicious about it. But if you're asking whether I had a role in it, yes, I suppose I did. I didn't do anything to stop her, and I should've. But hindsight is twenty-twenty, I guess."

"What should you have done?"

Betsy's laughter was high pitched and unnerving. "Why do you want to know all of this now?"

"Because I have to know the truth."

"Even if I tell you, I'll deny it all day long. It'll be your word against mine." It sounded like a caution.

"I don't care. It doesn't matter if anyone else believes me or not."

Betsy seemed to consider what she'd said. "Okay, fine. I guess you should know—she was your mother, after all. And I liked her. The fact is, I should've put a stop to the rumours that she was crazy. I should've owned up to killing Mary Brown first thing, and then none of it would've happened. But I didn't, and things worked out the way they did. And that's the end of it."

Beatrice gasped. "You? What?"

"You didn't know? I thought for sure you'd figured out that part," Betsy rasped, laughing and then erupted into a hacking cough. "Not as clever as you thought you were, huh?"

"I didn't think it could be true. I suspected it, but I couldn't believe it." Adrenaline surged through Bea's veins. Her thoughts were clear and steady now. She had put herself in a dangerous situation. She scanned the room for the fastest way out of there.

"It's true. Your mother said the same thing—she figured it out and no one believed her then, like no one will believe you now. They can't comprehend that a nice old lady like me could do something so heinous. But people do whatever they have to do to protect their family. Even kill."

Bea frowned. "You'd kill to protect a brother who impregnated a teenaged girl?"

"I could've gone either way on that — I didn't like what he did. I told him when we got here that he needed to control himself. I didn't want any trouble. Trouble was the last thing we could afford. But of course, he couldn't manage to keep it together long enough for us to establish a life for ourselves."

"Why did you have to run from your husband?"

"He was a dangerous man, a criminal. He robbed banks and jewellery stores. He mixed with the worst kind of thugs, and he was violent to me and Frank. So, when I got the chance, I stole from him and fled the country. I thought he'd be angry, but I didn't understand how long he'd look for us. This island saved our lives, that's the truth. No one came looking for us here. He spent decades scouring the earth for a sign of either one of us. And he never did find us."

"What did you steal?"

"A few things he'd taken from someone else. It doesn't matter. It paid for this shop and our house, our new life, our identities. The money gave us a chance to start over, and I'd do it all again if I had to. It was worth it. Mary found out that Buck was the father of Ruby's baby, and she threatened to go to the police, saying it was rape. Of course, I pointed out that sixteen wasn't considered rape in this state, but she said she knew it'd started earlier, and I couldn't fault her on that. But the problem was, if she went to the police, they'd look deeper into our past, and I couldn't afford for them to do that. 'Course, that was before I made good friends down at the station, friends who like to help me avoid too much scrutiny for a bit of back-scratching."

"Back-scratching?"

"Never mind, honey. You're too naïve to understand how the world works. But let's say I was desperate, and I found a way to make sure Mary never went to the police with her sad tale. Ruby was too afraid to go herself after Mary's death. So, it all worked out."

Anger stirred in Bea's gut. "It didn't work out for Penny's family."

"No, you're right about that. But I was more concerned with protecting my own family at the time. I didn't think much about how things would progress. I was new to the island, and I didn't know many people. Of course, now they're like family to me, so I'd probably handle things differently given the chance to do it over."

"You let your own brother take the blame for the murder..."

"I figured he owed me, after what he'd done. He could've blown our cover and gotten all of us killed, the lout. He never was much of a thinker. I brought him with us to keep him safe and so he could help us in case we needed it, but I should've left him behind. He brought nothing with him but trouble."

Bea strode to the door, then spun on her heel and marched back to where Betsy sat. "You talk about murder as though it's nothing. No big deal. But you ended someone's life. You destroyed families—mine and Penny's. My mother never got over the way people treated her. She discovered the truth, and everyone called her crazy for it."

"I felt bad about that. Truly, I did." Betsy's black eyes glittered cunningly.

Bea didn't believe a word. "You've never felt bad about a thing in your life."

Betsy grinned. "Now, you could be right about that. I *want* to feel bad, but I'm not sure I do."

"What about the evidence in the cave? Whose blouse was that?"

"Mary's, of course."

"Why didn't the police match the DNA?"

"No DNA back then, was there? I'm sure if there's any left on it, they're matching it to her grandchildren now. But they haven't said a thing to me about it, and I'm not sure how those things work. It'll likely be used in the case against my brother when the time comes, if they manage it."

"You'll let him take the fall?"

"I haven't decided on that yet. I'm thinking about it." Betsy tapped a finger to her chin, as though lost in deep thought. "Maybe. Maybe not."

Bea glared at Betsy. "You're unhinged, a sociopath."

Betsy shrugged. "It's possible. But I'm also a mother and a grandmother, a sister, and a friend. Everything I've done has been to keep the people I love safe. And I'm sure you'd do the same."

"I'd never kill someone or let another person take her life because she was made to think she was crazy over my crimes."

"You don't know what you might do until you're in the situation. When you're worried about your baby, you might do almost anything at all."

"Why are you telling me this? You know I'll report it."

Betsy inhaled a slow breath. "Sometimes a load can get a bit too heavy to carry for another mile. I don't want to carry this secret any longer. It's time to let it go. Besides, as I said before, maybe no one will believe you. Don't be like your mother — move on with your life. It'll be best for you and for the island if we can put this drama to bed and let it rest."

Beatrice's nostrils flared. She wanted to scream, shout, slap that silly half-smile off Betsy's wrinkled old face. Instead, she spun on her heel and stormed from the shop. She was half infuriated and half scared to death. She hadn't been certain that Betsy would let her leave after baring her soul that way. She was afraid she'd pull out a knife or chase her down. But she wasn't a young woman any longer, and maybe what she'd said was true. Why would anyone believe that Betsy would simply open up and share her crimes the way she had? Regardless, Bea had to do what she could — she'd make an appointment to see the detective in charge of the case. He'd surely listen to her this time. There was no way he could ignore her now.

Eleven

THE ENTIRE CORNER of Main Street opposite the dock no longer held Bea's Coffee and Eveleigh's Books. Instead, the corner had been transformed into a sleek, modern, almost entirely white tourist office. Charmaine marched down Main Street, a book of floral arrangements beneath one arm, and stared agape at the new construction. She'd already seen it dozens of times, but today it was open, and she was going inside. There was something appealing about the sparkling glass windows and the gleaming white paint she hadn't noticed before, even if the entire building was a stark reminder of what had been lost.

The construction was finally complete. Evie and Bradford had been there all morning moving office equipment into the space, according to Evie. She'd called Charmaine earlier to ask her to come over with some ideas for a regular flower delivery for the office.

She spied Evie through the window. Her red curls were piled on top of her head, and she wore a pair of denim overalls and a pink shirt beneath it. Knee-high pink-striped socks completed the ensemble. She looked cute, young, and carefree as she waved to Charmaine.

The front door was ajar, so Charmaine stepped inside, scanning the room as she went. She marvelled at how new and perfect every aspect of the office was.

"This is amazing," she said.

"Does it look like a hospital? I told Bradford we need a bit more colour."

"You can add accents, but this is great," Charmaine replied. "I love it. Very streamlined."

"That's true," Evie replied. "Not my style, but then it's not about me. I'm only the employee."

"How is everything coming together?" Charmaine asked, sitting in a chair and crossing her legs.

Evie sat across from her. "It's going well. The construction was only a couple of weeks behind schedule. Bradford has taken the boat back to the mainland to get another load of supplies to bring over, and we're on track to open in a few days' time. It's going to be scary, but I'm looking forward to it."

"Do you think you'll enjoy being a tourist guide?" Charmaine asked.

"I really do. Brad has already promised to teach me how to scuba dive and sail, so eventually I can take customers out on tours and not be stuck behind the desk. But for now, I'm going to learn the business here, in the office."

"I'm kind of jealous, I have to admit," Charmaine replied with pursed lips.

"Jealous? Why?"

"You get to work with Brad all day, every day."

Evie laughed. "He won't be here much. He's mostly at the main office or out on the yachts."

"Still..."

"I promise to make sure no one flirts with him," Evie whispered conspiratorially.

Charmaine hid a smile behind her hand. "I've never had such a good looking boyfriend before, and I'm not used to all the stares he gets. I still don't know what he sees in me."

Evie waved a hand. "Oh, stop with that nonsense. You're a great catch. He sees how lovely you are. He's a smart guy."

"Halloooo?" Bea's voice echoed through the open space. She angled her head through the doorway, and her gaze met Charmaine. Her cheeks were flushed, her hair messy. Her eyes were glassy, and she blinked repeatedly.

Charmaine stood to her feet. "Are you okay, Bea?"

Bea hurried inside, shut the door behind her, and glanced out the window, peering as best she could around the two women. "Can we pull the blinds on those windows?"

Evie frowned. "Um... Sure, okay." She closed the blinds on the line of windows with one push of a button against the wall. The blinds whirred shut slowly until the women stood in darkness.

"Light switch?" Bea's voice rang out.

"By the door," Evie replied.

The shop sprang to life with the lights overhead flickering on all at once. Bea strode across the floor and stopped in front of Charmaine and Evie.

"I have to tell you something, but we're all going to need a stiff drink. What can we drink, Evie?"

Evie glanced around the shop strewn with half-empty boxes and pieces of semi-finished furniture. "Well... I think there's some kombucha in the kitchen."

"That will have to do," Bea replied.

Evie hurried to pour three glasses of kombucha and brought them back on a tray beside a pile of crackers and cheese on a very white brand-new plate.

"Everything's white, huh?" Bea asked.

"White, white, white," Evie replied with crossed eyes. "Your brother loves it. I'm coming around. Chaz thinks I can add splashes of colour."

Bea laughed. "Good luck with that. Let's sit. You're not going to believe what happened."

* * *

By the time Bea had finished telling Charmaine and Evie what Betsy had said and done, Charmaine could barely contain herself. She leapt to her feet and paced to the windows, then back again.

"She told you all this stuff?"

"Yep, blurted it out like she's been wanting to spill for a long time and was glad someone finally asked."

"That's so strange," Evie replied, her eyes wide and staring blankly at the ground. "How could Betsy kill anyone? She's so nice."

"I don't think she's very nice. Stabbing someone to death puts a bit of a damper on the whole *nice-old-lady* image." Bea shook her head. "What kind of person...?"

"Clearly a psychopath," Evie said.

Charmaine paced some more. "But ... it doesn't make sense. And yet it does. I still can't believe it. She's my boss, my friend. I've come to see her as family, since I lost my own. And now? Now what?" A lump built rapidly in her throat. This couldn't be happening.

Bea hurried to her side. "I'm sorry—I wasn't thinking. Of course you'd be upset. I shouldn't have told you—at least, not like that. I'm so shocked about the whole thing; I'm not seeing things clearly."

"It's not your fault," Charmaine murmured. "Only I still can't take it in."

"She wasn't this old, you know. At the time, she only

would've been about thirty. She could've done it," Evie said with a sigh. "It was a long time ago."

"That's true," Charmaine admitted, the lump in her throat growing. She didn't want to cry. It was silly to cry because a murderer had turned out not to be the nice person you thought they were. Silly and embarrassing. She held back the tears with a cough.

"We were all fooled," Bea said, patting Charmaine's back. "It's true that you didn't see it, but none of us did. We all love Betsy. The whole island adores her. She's part of the furniture around here—a fact she reminded me of. She said no one would believe me if I told them she admitted to the murder. Still, I'm going to the police. If they don't believe me, I'll deal with that when it happens."

"Well, I believe you," Evie said.

"Me too," Charmaine whispered. "I don't want to, but I do."

"Thank you," Bea said with a shake of her head. Her brow furrowed. "But can I ask why you believe me, Chaz? You love Betsy. You've told us before you can't believe she'd be part of this, yet now you're ready to accept that I haven't made this story up. That it's all true, even though it means your friend and boss is a murderer. Has something changed?"

Charmaine didn't want to say it, but she had to. There was no keeping it to herself now. And if she didn't speak up, she'd be putting herself in harm's way. It was time to bring everything out into the open, no matter what the consequences might be.

"I know you're telling the truth because my mother witnessed the murder."

"What?" Evie bounded to her feet. "What are you talking about? Who is your mother?"

"My mother was Helen Hilton."

81

Bea stared at her, blinking. Evie pressed her hands to her forehead as tears filled her eyes. "You're Helen's daughter?"

Charmaine nodded.

Evie and Bea exchanged a glance. Tears snaked down Evie's cheeks, and Bea sat suddenly with a huff of air and looked blankly at the wall ahead of her.

Charmaine felt lighter. Most of her secrets had been uncovered. It'd been so long since she'd been able to open up to anyone in her life. All this time she'd kept the truth close to her chest, guarding it as though anything else might leave her bereft of security. But now that it was out, there was no pushing it back in. It was time to tell them everything.

Twelve

IT TOOK a long while before Beatrice and Evie finally stopped asking questions. Charmaine did her best to give the answers they wanted. This was all new for her — opening up and sharing information about her family and their history wasn't something she'd ever been comfortable doing.

Perhaps she shouldn't have told them. It was a lot for them to take in, and they were more emotional than she'd thought they would be. Clearly they'd known her mother, but whether that was a good or bad thing, she couldn't quite tell yet.

Bea cleared her throat and blew her nose on a tissue, then walked over to Charmaine and threw her arms around her, holding her tight. Evie followed, squeezing both in a bear hug that left Charmaine breathless. They stood that way for several long seconds. Then Evie stepped back to blow her nose again, and Bea let go to peer directly into Charmaine's eyes.

"Yes, you have her eyes. And her nose. I don't know why I didn't see it before now."

"You knew her?"

"Of course we did," Bea replied. "She was a few years older

than us, of course. We looked up to her. She was so much fun and a great athlete. I still remember watching her do the one-hundred-metre sprint when I was in year seven and she was in year twelve."

"She was amazing," Evie sighed. "And then after school, we became friends. The gaps between the years close when you're older."

"I was gone, back to the city by then," Bea said. "But Evie was here for a little while."

"Then I left as well," Evie said. "And when I returned years later, your mother was already divorced and had left town with the kids. When I asked her parents and sister about it, they were tight-lipped and wouldn't tell me where she'd gone. It's been a mystery on the island for decades. Whatever happened to Helen? Her sister Finn is still here — have you met her yet?"

"Yes, I met her. She's the reason I came to Coral Island. I wanted to find her," Charmaine said, sliding back into her chair. "Anyway, I shared that with you because I know where some of the jewellery is that Betsy stole from her thieving husband."

Bea ceased blowing her nose and stared at Charmaine in wonder. "Where is it?"

"It's in the bank vault. My mother found it in a cave, I'm assuming it might've been the one near your beach cottage, and she kept it hidden all these years. Betsy tried to steal it back —I guess it was Betsy, although it could've been Buck, I suppose. Someone broke into Mum's house and then into my grandparents' house repeatedly looking for it. I think it's worth a lot of money. But I've got it now—I found it after Mum died. In fact, that's why my brother was here — he got wind of it and wanted to take it. So I put it in the bank vault, where it's safe. But I think we should take it to the police when you go. It's evidence, and it'll probably help put Betsy away. They'll believe your story if we have the diamonds, won't they?"

"If we have the diamonds with us, they'll have to," Bea stated with an emphatic nod.

Thirteen

TAYA BUSTLED about the dining room setting silverware in place, fixing a folded napkin, rearranging the vase of flowers. She shouldn't be nervous — lunch with the girls used to be a regular affair. But it'd been so long since all four of them had gathered, she felt butterflies in the pit of her stomach. She'd missed Penny so much. With everything that'd been going on in her life, having her sweet friend nearby to encourage and support her would've been exactly what she needed. But there was no use worrying about it now because that wasn't to be. Penny lived abroad with her husband, traveling for the stories he covered, and that was their new reality. Taya simply had to deal with it.

Bea was the first to arrive, with Evie close behind.

"I can't believe you parked that way," Evie said, out of breath as she jogged to catch up.

"What? It's fine." Bea brushed her aside, giving Taya a kiss on the cheek. "Let it go."

"You're at an angle. You have to redo it or someone will run into the side of your truck."

"Aidan's truck, and I'm sure no one will dent it. We're in Blue Shoal—there's hardly any traffic at the busiest of times."

Evie shook her head. "You're a rebel and a rule breaker, Beatrice Rushton."

"Whitlock now," Bea reminded her with a twinkle in her eye. "I finally changed my name."

"I'm not sure I'll ever get used to that," Taya said with a sigh. "'Old dogs and new tricks' springs to mind. I've called you Beatrice Rushton my entire life."

Bea shrugged.

Evie gave Taya a hug, then the three of them sat at the table.

"Where's Penny? I thought *we* were running late," Evie said, glancing around.

"She'll be here. And you're not late. Not really."

Beatrice linked her hands together on top of the table. "There's something you should know before she gets here..."

Bea seemed uncomfortable, her cheeks pinker than usual. What was going on?

Just then, Penny arrived, carrying an armload of wrapped gifts. She set them all on the table. "Ta-da! I'm home!"

She grinned, looking around at each of the women, her arms open wide for a hug. But no one moved. All eyes were glued to her enormous stomach. Taya gaped like a goldfish. Her mouth opened and closed, but no sound emerged.

Penny looked down at her bump. "Oh, I thought Bea would've told you."

Beatrice stood and embraced Penny with a warm smile. "I was about to, and you interrupted us. Rude." She laughed.

Penny bit down on her lower lip. "I wanted to surprise you. So, what do you think? Come on, Taya. I know you have something to say."

Taya's eyes filled with tears. She strode over to Penny and

wrapped her arms around her friend. "I can't believe it. Congratulations, sweetie."

That's when Evie began to sniffle, hiccoughing through a veil of tears. "When are you due?" She hugged Penny next.

"I'm due in two months. Although, look at the size of me. You'd think I was popping tomorrow. The doctor says I have a short body. Not exactly a news flash." She laughed, rubbing one hand over her distended stomach.

They each took a seat at the round dining table in the private dining room of the Blue Shoal Inn. The place was warm and familiar to Taya after many years as the owner. But the dining room had been updated, and she hadn't worked there in more than twelve months. It still reminded her of Dad.

She didn't seem to be able to stop crying. Tears streaked down her cheeks, and she sat in silence, not wanting to ruin the moment for Penny but unable to do anything about it.

"Oh, honey, are you okay?" Penny asked, coming around to where she sat and kneeling beside her.

Taya nodded, still crying quietly. "I'm fine. Don't kneel there—you might not be able to get up again."

Penny laughed and lumbered to her feet. "You're right about that." She pulled up a chair. "Is it your dad?"

"I guess so. I'm a mess. I've been crying nonstop for over a week. I can't seem to get a handle on my emotions."

"I know how much you miss him."

"I do, but I'm also happy for you. That's why I'm crying now. Because I'm emotional, but also because I never thought I'd see..." She burst into tears again, unable to continue.

Penny leaned forward to hug Taya. Then Bea and Evie came over and joined them. They all sat together for a long time in a warm embrace until finally Taya's tears dried and she was able to speak again.

"We should eat," she said. "If there's food in my mouth, I can't cry."

They all laughed and took their seats again. The table was covered with plates of appetisers — cheeses, crackers, olives and thinly sliced deli meats. They filled up their plates with the good food and sipped iced tea.

"You know there's nothing wrong with a good cry," Evie said as she placed a napkin in her lap.

"I sometimes cry at commercials," Bea added. "They make them so emotional these days."

"Me too," Penny admitted. "Of course, more so now that I'm pregnant. The hormones have been a killer."

"How are you feeling generally?" Evie asked.

Penny smirked. "Pretty good. Though they call me a geriatric mother. Did you know that? Kind of rude, if you ask me."

Taya's brow furrowed. "Very rude. You're not geriatric."

"I'm forty-seven, almost forty-eight."

"Which begs the question," Bea said. "How?"

Penny laughed and shook her head so her blonde curls bounced. "We weren't trying or anything. The doctor said it can happen, obviously, but it's very rare."

"It's a miracle," Evie said. "I bet you were surprised."

"That doesn't even come close to covering it," Penny replied. "I was in utter shock. Plus, I felt awful all the time. I was so tired. I was convinced I had cancer, so I went to the doctor and almost fell off my chair when he told me I was pregnant."

"How does Rowan feel?" Taya asked.

Penny grinned. "He's over the moon. Neither of us ever had children, and we didn't think we would get the chance. Now, it feels like everything is different. We have more to worry about than ourselves. We've got to plan a future for our child. It's so strange to say that."

A waiter came into the room to take their orders. Taya unfolded the napkin to place in her lap. "Well, I think we can safely say you will be the only pregnant alumnus at our high school reunion."

They all laughed heartily at that.

* * *

After the main course arrived—roast beef with crispy roasted vegetables and fresh greens with gravy on top—the ladies dug in while chatting about everything that'd happened in each of their lives since their last get-together.

"How do you like life on the road?" Taya asked. She'd spoken to Penny about it before, of course. But now that her friend was pregnant, she wondered if anything had changed.

"It's fun. We've had the best time. It was a good move for our marriage and for our mental health. Especially for Rowan's, of course. He's back to his old self—confident, obnoxious, happy."

"And you?" Evie asked.

"I'm better," Penny replied. "I'm lonely, of course. And I get bored. I've read a lot of books, watched a lot of movies, but maybe that was what I needed. I was feeling pretty run down before we left. But that was the other thing I wanted to talk to all of you about — we've decided that I should move back home to Coral Island while Rowan stays out on the road. For now, anyway."

"Really?" Taya asked.

"Yes. Travelling isn't great for me when I'm pregnant. I get sick a lot more often when we're on the move. Plus, restaurant food is so rich, I've struggled with indigestion. And some of the places we're going aren't very safe."

"You're moving home?" Bea exclaimed.

Penny nodded. "I'm moving home."

A surge of happiness washed over Taya. It lifted the mantle of sadness. "That's the best news I've heard in a while. Well, that and the baby. You're going to be here, and we can give you a shower and watch the baby grow and see his or her first steps. I'm so excited."

"That's great news, honey," Evie added.

"Will you go back to work at the animal refuge?" Bea asked.

Penny sighed. "I'd like to, but we've decided to leave the manager in place. Her contract isn't finished, and besides, I'll want to have maternity leave soon anyway. So, I'll oversee things, but I won't be on site every day or anything like that. And once the baby is a bit older, we can revisit it all and decide where to go from there."

"That sounds like a great plan," Taya replied. "But how long will Rowan work on the road?"

Penny's smile faded. She swallowed. "Indefinitely. He doesn't want to give up his career. We tried that, and it didn't go well. He was so unhappy. I think there were a lot of factors involved, but he doesn't agree. He knows that he's feeling better now than he was before, and he doesn't want that to change. It's fine, though. I don't mind. I want him to be happy. It means we'll be apart sometimes, and he'll fly home whenever he can. But I don't want to live on the road."

"You do whatever works for you," Bea replied.

Taya took a bite of roast beef and chewed thoughtfully. Everything was changing, some things for the better. Life lately had been an emotional roller coaster ride. She was grateful for Penny's pregnancy and that she was moving home. She worried that Penny and Rowan's marriage might not survive their living apart, but they would deal with that when it happened—if it happened. If they could find a healthy balance for themselves, who was she to criticise?

"How are you coping with everything, Taya?" Evie asked as she took a sip of iced tea.

Taya's stomach clenched. Whenever anyone wanted to talk about her dad, she felt nothing but dread and anguish. "I'm coping. Mum's strangely serene. I'm worried she's in denial. But we're putting together a lovely public memorial service for Friday. I knew Dad had impacted a lot of lives, but I'm surprised every day by how many notes, letters, bunches of flowers and phone calls Mum gets from people all over the world. So many people want to pay their respects, so we thought this would be the best way. You're invited, by the way. It's at the chapel here in Blue Shoal."

"We'll be there," Bea replied.

"Are you going with your mum or Andrew, Taya?" Penny asked.

Taya hesitated. "I'll be with Mum. Andrew broke up with me."

"What?" All three ladies exclaimed the word in unison.

Bea held a cup in the air, Evie sputtered around a mouthful of potato, and Penny set her fork down on her plate, her cheeks growing redder by the moment.

"He broke up with you?" Penny asked, her eyes narrow.

Taya pressed her lips into a thin line. "Yesterday."

"Three weeks after your father's death, and he breaks up with you?"

Taya nodded. "He says his parents are coming to stay with him to escape some kind of religious extremists who killed his wife years ago. And they're traditionalists who won't understand our relationship."

"That's ridiculous," Penny huffed. "What's to understand? You care for each other."

"I thought we did," Taya replied. "It turns out I was wrong, I guess."

"That was cruel of him," Bea said. "I never would've imagined he could do something like that."

"C'est la vie," Taya replied. "But I don't want to talk about it. I've only just stopped crying, and we've got a delicious roast to eat. Let's talk about something lively and fun. Like, whether we should have a theme for the reunion."

"A theme?" Bea asked. "I hadn't thought about that."

"We could do *Alice in Wonderland*," Evie suggested.

"Or what about Sherlock Holmes?" Penny said.

Taya tipped her head to one side. "Sherlock Holmes? That might be interesting. People could dress up as him, a police officer, or a criminal."

"It could be fun. But do people like going to dress-up parties these days?" Bea asked, her tone sceptical.

"I don't know," Taya replied. "But I think we should do it. We're having a scavenger hunt—we can set it up to match the theme."

"That's a great idea."

"But how about something more applicable to the event, like nineties?" Evie suggested.

"I love it," Taya replied.

"Grunge rock, plaid and torn jeans," Bea said with a laugh.

"Doc Martens," Evie added.

"And don't forget denim jackets," Taya said.

"Only one problem," Bea said miserably. "I haven't been able to think of anything for the scavenger hunt. I need help with ideas."

"Let's get together and come up with a plan," Evie replied. "It'll be great."

Fourteen

BEATRICE DIDN'T OFTEN DO her grocery shopping in Kellyville these days since she lived over in Point Prospect now with Aidan, but she'd come to Kellyville because the butcher there had the best corned beef on the island, and she wanted to cook corned beef with mashed potatoes and cauliflower with cheese sauce for dinner.

Penny and Rowan were coming over, and she needed everything to be perfect. She wasn't sure exactly why she felt that need, but she did. It was almost as though she wanted to impress Rowan so he'd stay on the island and be nice to her friend. But of course, she couldn't control that, and certainly not with a delicious dinner menu. There were a lot of things she couldn't control in life—she'd learned that well enough over the years. But one thing she could control was the corned beef she chose for dinner, and so she intended to buy the best one and cook it as perfectly and precisely as she could manage.

She manoeuvred her cart full of groceries down the street towards her car. For some reason, she'd managed to find the only cart available with a bum wheel, and it kept veering off to the right. It was laden down with groceries, since she could never manage to pass a grocery store without stocking up on much needed items, and it took all her core strength to keep it on track and away from the gutter.

That was when she spotted Sean. Or at least, she thought she did. Charmaine's brother wasn't someone she knew well. She'd only seen him a couple of times while he lived on the island. But she spied a man from a distance as he ducked around a corner up ahead, and she could've sworn it was him.

As soon as the thought flitted through her mind, she convinced herself that no, it wasn't Sean—it was someone else. Surely Sean wouldn't return to Coral Island while he was wanted by the Coral Island police. But even as she continued driving the trolley towards the car, straining to keep it on the footpath, she couldn't get the idea out of her mind. She decided she would go to the police station and tell them what she thought she'd witnessed. At least then it wouldn't be on her shoulders anymore. It'd be their problem to deal with.

It was a humid day, and sweat trickled down the sides of her face as she loaded the groceries into her car. Then she locked it up, noting that she couldn't be long since the cold storage bag would only keep the meat cool for a limited amount of time in that heat, even with the frozen bricks she'd brought with her, and headed for the police station.

Inside the station, the air-conditioning cooled her over-heated body down gradually as she waited in the reception area. She was ushered through the building to a small office, where a rotund man with a comb-over was eating a sandwich, a drop of mayonnaise on his tie. He glanced up at her in surprise, then beckoned her into the office to take a seat opposite him at his desk.

"Come in," he said as soon as he'd managed to swallow his last bite. "Take a seat. What can I do for you, Mrs...?"

"Whitlock. I'm Beatrice Whitlock. We've met before. I gave a statement a while ago about some evidence I found in the Buck Clements case in that cave hidden in the cliff-face. Also, I was the owner of the cafe that burned down."

"Oh, yes, of course. Ms Whitlock, it's nice to see you again. What can I do for you today?"

He wiped his mouth and his tie with a napkin, then his gaze rested on Bea's.

"I thought you might like to know that I saw Sean Billings on Main Street. At least, I think I did. I'm not sure—he wasn't very close to me, but not too far either. Anyway, it was only a few minutes ago. If you hurry, you might see him…"

"You might or might not have seen who now?"

"Sean Billings," she offered, confused. "Aren't you looking for him — to question him about the fire at the café and bookshop?"

"Yeah, that's right. I didn't recognise the name right away. You saw him, you say?"

"I think so. Anyway, I thought you might like to know. I have a roast in my car, so I must get going."

He stood to his feet and moved to open the office door for her. Then he cocked his head to one side. "Do you know Sean well?"

"No. I've met him twice, I believe."

"But you think you'd recognise him if you saw him?"

"I would. His face isn't easily forgotten, given it was probably him who burned my business to the ground."

"Well, we don't know that," the detective crooned with a patronising tone. "Let's not get ahead of ourselves now."

His attitude bothered Bea. "I'm curious to know why that's getting ahead of ourselves, Detective. Don't you have any leads in this case or any idea who did it? It's been a while now. I would've expected you to make some progress."

He cleared his throat. "We've got some ideas and some evidence. As you know, the official finding was that the fire was accidental. But I would certainly like to speak with Sean about the incident if you see him again."

"I thought you might like to look for him. You know, do some investigating." She knew her tone was too sarcastic, that she would likely do nothing more than put the man offside, but she couldn't seem to help herself. The police had done almost nothing to try to find the person who'd burned down both the café and the bookshop. The crime had been devastating to her and to Evie. They'd lost so much in such a short space of time, and here was the lead detective, unable to recognise the chief suspect's name and showing no interest whatsoever in the fact that she might've seen him in the street outside the station only a few moments earlier.

He leaned back on his heels. "I see."

"Also, my friends and I have some information in the Mary Brown case. We'd like to talk to you about it. I made an appointment with your assistant, but she couldn't find a time until next week. Would it be possible to come in sooner? I think you'll find our evidence quite compelling."

He eyed her with curiosity and a little irritation. "Tomorrow at ten is fine."

"I'll see you then. Thank you, Detective..."

"Mooney."

"Thank you, Detective Mooney."

* * *

The next day, Bea, Charmaine and Evie all gathered for a coffee at the dock before heading to the police station together. On the way there, they stopped by the bank. Charmaine took a photograph of the jewellery on her phone, then put it back in her lock box.

Inside the station, Bea's fingers drummed out a steady

rhythm on the arm of her chair. Evie chewed a fingernail. Charmaine sat opposite Bea and stared at the floor by her feet.

"Come with me," a cheerful woman said.

They followed her to Detective Mooney's office, and each took a seat against the wall. He wasn't there, but came in soon after carrying a cup of tea on a saucer. He set the saucer down on his desk and went to shake hands with each of the women. His demeanour was much friendlier than it had been the day before when it was only Bea in his office.

"Welcome, ladies. How nice to see you. Can I offer you a drink?"

"No, thank you," Evie said. "We've had one."

"Beatrice told me you have something to share with me. A statement to make in the Mary Brown case?"

He glanced from one woman to the other. His gaze finally landed on Bea.

She nodded. "Thank you for seeing us, Detective. We have a story to tell that I think you'll enjoy."

By the time Bea had finished relaying what Betsy had told her and Charmaine had woven her own tale of the events of her life and shown the photographs of stolen jewellery, the detective's attitude had become more serious and pensive. He called for another detective to come into the room, and between them, they had the women repeat everything from the beginning in a formal recorded statement.

"One of the keys to breaking the case was that Betsy had photographs of herself pinned up behind the cash register in the florist shop," Charmaine explained. "Taken with famous people."

"How did she know so many of them, I wonder?" Bea asked.

"I imagine her former husband had relationships with a lot of powerful people," Detective Mooney mused. "From what you've told me."

Had Detective Mooney already discovered Betsy's true identity when investigating the case? It seemed like he knew more than he'd let on to them. Regardless, the truth was out in the open now, and Bea was glad. It was no longer her burden to carry.

Finally, Detective Mooney sat back in his chair, hands linked behind his head, and sighed. "Well, that's a lot more detail than I would've thought possible. Well done, ladies. You make fine detectives."

"Will you arrest Betsy?" Bea asked.

The two detectives exchanged a glance. "We'll need to get a warrant from a judge on the mainland, and that might not happen for a few days. But there is something we can tell you that might give you a bit more understanding of the situation. Before you came into the station today, Frank Norton visited and informed us that Betsy Norton, his mother, is missing."

Fifteen

THE POOL IN HER PARENTS' backyard had always been a place of sanctuary and rest for Taya. She swam a lazy lap down the length of it, then did a somersault turn at the end and swam back again. A splash caught her attention and she stood up with a start, her feet scrambling for a foothold on the concrete bottom of the pool.

"Mum, you almost landed on me," she stuttered before coughing up pool water.

Her mother's hair was wet and plastered down against her head. She giggled and used one hand to splash Taya in the face. With mock horror, Taya gaped, then splashed her back. Pretty soon, they were engaged in an all-out water fight, Taya hiding behind a large blow-up swan and her mother alternating between ducking beneath the water and emerging like a slow-motion superhero to rain down more water on Taya's exposed head.

After a while, Taya was exhausted and raised both hands in surrender, laughing so hard that she could barely speak. "Okay, Mum, stop. I'm going to keel over if I don't catch my breath soon."

Her mother was panting as well. They both climbed out of the pool and lay on banana lounges in the shade to calm their heart rates.

"You do pretty well for an old lady," Taya quipped.

Mum crossed her eyes and poked out her tongue. "Old! Gah. I'm not old. I go to Pilates three times a week and walk five kilometres every morning."

"You're amazing," Taya said with a sigh. "You're in great shape, Mum. And I mean that in more ways than one. I don't know how you're coping so well, but I'm surprised. I thought for sure you'd fall apart without Dad."

"Why would I do that?" Mum asked, tenting a hand over her eyes to meet Taya's gaze.

It was mid-morning, and the sun was bright and hot in the sky overhead. It was a beautiful day, the kind of day that Taya felt bad for enjoying without her father there with her. How was Mum so okay, when she was his wife?

"I don't know. I suppose I was wrong about you. You're stronger than I knew."

Mum drew in a slow, deep breath, shut her eyes as the breath released back into the air around her. When she spoke, her voice was so soft that Taya almost couldn't hear it. "When we were first married, I thought I'd hit the jackpot. He was so handsome and kind, fun and cheeky. We had the best time together. I was in love. But then, he started this company of his and things changed. He was gone all the time, and I hardly ever saw him. At first, it broke my heart, but then I got used to it. I had to."

"You're used to him not being around," Taya said, realisation dawning. "I suppose that makes sense."

"In a way, but that's not what I'm saying. There were years when I had to manage everything on my own. He wasn't here, and even when he was, he was busy, and his thoughts were elsewhere. The house, the bills, the groceries, clothing—all of it was my responsibility. He was like a house guest who came to visit when he had the chance. Oh, don't get me wrong. I loved him, but I had to learn not to rely on him or my heart would've broken every single time he flew off to open another resort location."

Taya peered up at the sky. A single pelican flew by overhead. Its giant wings flapped in a steady beat. There was no panic, no anxiety, no rush. The bird knew it had time between each beat of its wings; it wouldn't fall to the ground. It trusted the wind that carried it forward to keep it aloft between each flap. Taya had never mastered that skill. She inhaled slowly, like her mother had done, and let the air flow back out through her mouth in a long, easy motion. The tension in her gut unravelled a little, and so she did it again.

"Then you came along," Mum continued. "And you never slept. You had colic, and you cried all night long. I thought I'd lose my mind." She chuckled. "But I didn't. I managed because I had to. There was no one to help me. Oh, I could've asked my mother to come, but she never had a kind word for me or your father, so I held my tongue and decided that I could do it alone."

"And you did," Taya said.

"Yes, I did. We got through the baby year, you and me. Your father was building the resort in Darwin, I believe. I learned how to be a mother, and you learned how to face the world without quite so much crying. We had a wonderful time together, even with all the sleepless nights. I loved being a mother — still do."

"You're a good mum," Taya said. "The best. I didn't always understand you, but I do more and more these days. And I couldn't have asked for anyone better to raise me. I think I blamed you sometimes for Dad's absence. I took it out on you, and I'm sorry for doing that."

Mum smiled. "It's okay. Water under the bridge."

"You were both wonderful parents to me."

"We did our best. You were our dream come true. I wanted more children. Did you know that?"

Taya shook her head, frowning. "Really?"

"Yep. I would've loved a whole lot of children all running around me, noisy and laughing and fighting and playing. It was my dream. But I couldn't have any after you. There was no real reason—at least none the doctors could find. I had secondary infertility, they said. What it meant was no more children and no one for you to play with. It broke my heart, but I coped. I became your pal, your playmate. I threw myself into raising you, took you to play group and music lessons, swimming lessons and crawling club. Everything I could find, we were part of it."

Taya laughed. "I remember being very busy after school some days — dance and piano, swimming and running."

"We did it all," Mum said as she chased a fly away with a bat of her hand.

"Thank you for such a great childhood. I often feel bad for anyone who didn't get to grow up on Coral Island."

"You had an idyllic childhood. One I would've loved to have. I gave you everything I could, everything I never had. Love, affection, encouragement, belief. I hope you know I still believe in you."

"I know that, Mum. You're a good cheerleader. But the thing is, I'm completely overwhelmed." Even as she spoke the words, a lump formed in her throat.

"Overwhelmed by what, honey?"

"Everything. Andrew broke up with me."

"I'm sorry to hear that." Mum stared at the sky. Her voice was monotone, as though she wasn't bothered by Taya's words.

"You don't sound very sorry," Taya snipped.

Mum shrugged. "I'm not surprised."

"What? That's not..."

"I mean, he wasn't right for you, honey. He isn't strong like you are. You're too much for him. It's not unusual for a man to break it off with a woman when things get real — like dealing with grief. Maybe he's had enough of grief in his life. Or perhaps he doesn't like being faced with real emotions. I don't know, but he was a lovely boyfriend, a nice man, someone to get you over the hump of dating again. That's not a tragedy, my love. That's an opportunity."

Taya had never seen this side of her mother before. "When did you become such a fount of wisdom?"

A half smile played around Mum's lips. "I've always been like this. I simply hide it beneath my passion for interior decorating and cross-stitch."

Taya guffawed in surprise. Mum had a sense of humour. Who knew?

"It's not only Andrew, although I'm angry at him for the timing of the breakup. But I miss Dad all the time. I regret the way I treated him all those years, the resentment I held on to about him being gone so much. I should've accepted him and enjoyed the times we had together. Now that's all gone, and I can't get it back. I can't change the way I spoke to him or the hurt I caused."

Mum patted her leg. "Oh, honey, he wasn't hurt by you. He was proud of you and loved you. Parents know their children are going to be angry sometimes. It comes with the territory. You have nothing to regret. Dad didn't hold on to any of it."

Tears slid down Taya's cheeks. "I know I have to let him go."

"You do, honey. Let him go. It's not a tragedy to say goodbye. He had a good life. He achieved everything he wanted to in this world. He raised a wonderful daughter, saw his granddaughter grow into adulthood. He told me last year that he was content to retire and leave the company in your hands, which is a very big deal for him."

"I'm not ready though," Taya said, wiping her eyes with her fingertips. "I don't know what I'm doing. I'm sure everyone can see that. They won't respect me the way they did Dad. I'm not him, and I don't know how to do what he did."

Mum sat up straight and looked Taya in the eye. "You don't have to be him or even be *like* him. Being yourself is good enough."

Taya rubbed both hands over her face with a groan. "What if I mess up? What if I destroy the company that took Dad his entire life to build? I could lose it all, Mum. What then?"

"Your father never meant his company to be a burden to you. He wanted it to be your birthright. The heritage he never got from his family — an inheritance on which you and Camden can build the kind of life you've always wanted."

Taya sat up as well, swinging her legs over the side of the lounger. "Are you sure? That company was his baby."

"No, *you* were his baby. The company was his pride and joy, but never more than you. We talked about it a lot in recent months — that he wanted you to enjoy the business, to have a happy, fulfilled life. He hoped it would be something you could pass on to Camden one day and maybe she can pass it on as well. A family business to span the generations — that was his dream."

"That's a lot of pressure, Mum." Taya tipped her head to one side and stretched the tension from her neck muscles, then did the other side. Her stomach clenched. Her father's dream depended upon her ability to manage a huge company, and she'd never done anything like that before.

"I needed more time to learn the business. To see how Dad operated. I hardly got the chance to work with him, and now he's gone."

"Taya, you're underselling yourself. You've watched him

operate your entire life. You know how to do this. You've got it inside you — the strength, resilience, confidence you need. Dad believed in you, and so do I. I'm not worried one bit. I've seen you at that little inn of yours managing the staff — who loved you, by the way. You somehow turned that tiny boutique inn into a profitable business for two decades all on your own. That's impressive, honey. If you can do that, you can do anything."

Mum went inside to mix up some mocktails for them to sip by the pool. Taya stretched her arms over her head, and dove back into the water. The cool blue of the pool swallowed her whole, easing her burgeoning headache and soothing the tension in her shoulders. She swam beneath the water to the end of the pool, then stood to her feet, puffing hard and leaning her back against the wall.

Perhaps Mum was right. Maybe she had everything she needed already buried deep inside her. Whenever she thought about the huge task ahead, she felt as though a wave was curling over her head, ready to smash her into the sand. But if she took one step at a time the way she'd always taught Camden when she was a little girl, she could manage it. She'd start by drafting that companywide email. It didn't have to be the kind of email her father would write—it could come from her heart. She was different from him, but they shared so much of the same blood and personality, skills, and gifts. She would bring a new flair to the role, but she understood how he worked. Her mother was right — she knew her father and what he'd say right now.

If he was standing in front of her, he'd cross his arms over his chest and grunt. "Pull it together, love. There's nothing stopping you from reaching your dreams, so go out and get them."

Sixteen

THE TOWER of flowers almost toppled to the ground, but Charmaine managed to keep her balance by tottering to the left and then the right. The flowers remained in their vases, and she didn't drop a single one. She shouldn't have taken so many vases at once from the florist shop, but she hadn't wanted to walk from there to the new Coral Island Tours office down the street more than once.

Bradford's company was having its official grand opening on the island, and Charmaine was responsible for the floral arrangements. She hadn't done any of the other organising since she was so busy working at the shop and planning the reunion as well as several upcoming weddings. She'd barely had time to see Bradford all week.

At the front door to the brand-new offices, she spun around and used her rear end to shove the doors inwards, then shuffled through the gap and into the offices. True to her word, Evie had warmed up the place with a few blue cushions, throw rugs, and pieces of art. She'd even purchased a matching trio of Charmaine's latest paintings.

The three paintings connected to form an impression of

the foreshore down by the docks. The dark timber of the dock contrasted with the pale golden sand and the clear azure water. There were pelicans dotted against the sand, and seagulls as slashes of white and grey hovering over the water. The paintings expressed how Charmaine felt about the island, how it was home to her and yet still so wild and remote. She was proud to see them hanging on the wall, and a lump formed in her throat.

She set the flowers down on a table.

"I'm here," Charmaine said. "I brought the flowers. Where would you like them?"

Evie greeted her. "Just in time! If you could place them around the space, I think it will look lovely. I've got the food table set up, the drinks in the corner over there, plenty of flyers... I think we're ready."

"It looks amazing," Charmaine said. "You've done a lot of work to get everything set up."

"Now, let's hope someone shows," Bradford added as he stepped through the front door.

He caught Charmaine in his arms and bent forward to kiss her.

Her face flushed with warmth. She wasn't accustomed to public displays of affection.

He stepped back, winding his fingers through hers. "I haven't seen nearly enough of you this week."

"I feel the same way. I still don't have any spare time today, but I had to make sure you have everything you need. I was able to duck out to help with your grand opening since Betsy hasn't come to work in days — I locked up the shop before I left and put the 'out to lunch' sign in the window. I'm sure no one will mind. But I'm getting a bit worried about her. The police told us she was missing, but I thought for sure she'd turn up. Have you seen her?"

Bradford shrugged. "Have you spoken to Frank yet?"

"No. I tried to call him, but he didn't answer."

"She's on the run, I guess," Evie said as she sorted flyers into stacks. "She confessed to Bea and then left town. We probably won't see her again."

"Confessed what to Bea?" Bradford asked, one eyebrow arched.

"That she killed Mary Brown."

"Betsy did?" Bradford gaped.

"Sorry, honey. I would've told you, but as we already established, I haven't seen you."

"I would never have guessed," Bradford said. "So, it wasn't Buck?"

"Apparently not," Evie replied.

A few people lined up outside. Bradford hurried to open the door and held it open with a stopper, then welcomed them all in. For the next hour, the tourists wandered in through the front doors of Bradford's new office, and he, Evie and Charmaine spoke to them about the services on offer—yacht rentals, deep sea fishing guides, coral reef snorkelling tours, and more. The Great Barrier Reef was an hour's boat ride away from Coral Island and was a big selling point for many of the tourists. Charmaine was ashamed to admit she'd never visited it herself. She hadn't been able to afford it.

Within an hour, she had to leave. There was too much to do and not enough hours in the day. She returned to the florist shop and got back to work. Several hours later, she was ready to finish up and decided to see if she could catch Bradford before he left for the day. Perhaps they could have dinner together.

She locked up and was walking along the street towards Bradford's new office when she remembered she hadn't balanced the till. She spun around to go back to the shop, when her high heel caught in a crack in the footpath. She staggered forward, out of balance, and almost landed in a patch of bright pink rhododendrons. Doing her best not to squash any of the plants, she stumbled away from the garden as a man sprinted past, almost knocking her to the ground.

When she looked up, she caught a glimpse of Sean's profile. He wore a pair of skinny jeans and a tight blue T-shirt. His hair was cut shorter and combed into a spiky style up top, but it was him. He wasn't the same greasy-haired gamer in stained, loose-fitting clothing who'd slept on her couch for months, but it was the same profile, the same brother she'd spent her whole life wishing she didn't love or care for as much as she did.

"Sean?"

He glanced over his shoulder, and his eyes found hers for a brief moment. Then he ducked down a side alley and was gone.

Maybe she'd imagined him. The entire event passed so quickly, it almost didn't seem real. No one else in the street seemed to care that Sean had sprinted by them on the footpath. Had it happened only in her mind? Just then, a police officer dressed in a smart navy-blue uniform turned the corner and looked up and down the street. He scanned the crowd, then spun on his heel and went back the way he'd come.

* * *

Later that evening, Charmaine woke to the sound of pounding on her door. The noise only confused her. Still woozy with sleep, she tried to get her bearings. With her face pressed firmly against her pillow, she groaned. Then she wiped the trail of saliva from her cheek, sat up, and blinked.

"Who is it?" she croaked.

Of course, they didn't hear her raspy whisper, so she had to move. She shuffled across the floor, into the hallway, and through the kitchen. When she opened the door, Bradford stood there with a covered bowl in his hands.

"This is hot," he said. "Let me put it down, and I'll give you a hug."

She hugged him. "It's the middle of the night, what are you doing here?"

"It's not the middle of the night, it's only ten o'clock. And I thought you were going to meet me for dinner."

"I was going to," she confirmed. "But..." She swallowed, unable to finish her thought.

He laughed. "I'm sorry, I didn't think you'd be asleep. You should go back to bed. I'll leave you alone."

He stepped inside the kitchen and set the bowl down on the bench. "I brought us laksa soup. But I see you're not coherent so I'll put it in the fridge."

"It's perfect. Thanks," Charmaine replied, shaking the sleep from her head. "And don't leave. I'll wake up. Let me get us some wine to drink and we can eat in a minute."

He put the soup on the bench, then watched as she opened a bottle of red wine and fetched glasses from the overhead cabinet.

"I'm glad you came over."

"I'm sorry I woke you."

"There are worse ways to wake up," she said, as she poured the wine into two glasses. "Besides, I'm absolutely famished. I was so busy today I hardly ate a thing, and then I fell into bed exhausted."

She handed one to him, then held up hers in a toast.

"Cheers."

"Cheers," he replied, tapping his glass against hers. "You know, you have sheet marks down one side of your face."

She touched her cheek with her fingers. "Hmmm... attractive."

He bit down on his lower lip to keep from laughing, his

brown eyes sparkling. "It is actually. It's very cute. I had no idea you were such an early bird."

"What can I say? I'm no good at staying up late. I like to sleep."

"I feel very much the same way. I love getting up early. It's the best time of day to be outside doing things."

"Oh, I don't like getting up early either. I'm someone who likes sleep in general," Charmaine said, sipping her wine slowly.

He chuckled. "Noted."

"How did your grand opening go?"

"It was fantastic. We have bookings through the next two weeks. I think this is going to expand the business."

She lowered herself into a chair. She wanted to lay her head on the table, but thought she should show at least some manners. After all, Bradford had already seen her with sheet face.

"Should we eat?" He asked.

She nodded, yawned wide.

He ladled laksa into two large bowls. The spicy soup was still hot and steam reached for the ceiling with winding tendrils.

"Thanks for being here," she said.

He nodded. "Nowhere else I'd rather be."

"I don't deserve you."

He laughed. "I hope you remember that."

"I'm serious."

"You deserve everything good."

"I think I saw Sean earlier," she said.

"What? Where?" Bradford's face clouded over.

"After work. He ran past me. I'm sure it was him, unless I was imagining things. And there was a police officer who followed, seemed to be looking for him."

"He's on Coral Island? I thought he agreed not to come back. Did he see you?"

"Yes," she replied. "Although I don't think he knows I've moved."

"I'm going to stay the night," Bradford replied, his brows pressed low over his dark eyes. "I don't trust that brother of yours. I know he's family, but he's trouble."

"I won't say no to that. He's always been trouble. I used to make excuses for him, and when you grow up with something your whole life, you start to believe it's normal. But now I know healthy, adult men who aren't grifters, and I can see him clearly for what he is. He's a criminal and a con man who only cares about himself."

"So, why is he back, then? You gave him what he wanted — the money he needed to pay off his debts. Isn't that what you told me?"

She took another sip. "I paid him a lot of money. It was his part of the house that we inherited from Mum. I want to keep it as an investment since I don't own any other real estate, so I took extra money out of the equity to pay him off. He's also getting a monthly portion of the rent I make, out of my own pocket, in exchange for him staying away from Coral Island."

"I guess you can stop making those payments to him now." Bradford's face was thunderous. "It still doesn't explain why he's here. Does he feel the need to destroy more of our lives before he leaves again?"

She hated the pain Sean had caused Bradford's family — his sister Bea had put her heart and soul into the café that Sean had most likely burned to the ground. The entire community had suffered the loss of delicious coffee and baked goods. Not to mention Evie's bookshop, which had been a staple business on the island for years.

"I'm sorry—this is all my fault. I should've known he would never stick to our agreement. I can't stay here. This will never end. He will keep coming back because he believes I have what he wants."

Bradford's eyes narrowed. "And what is that?"

She cleared her throat. "I wasn't going to tell you because I'm scared that whoever knows this secret might be in danger. As soon as word gets out about who I am, my real identity, I'll have to leave anyway since there's someone out there who has it in for me. I know who it is, but I'm not sure I should tell any of this to you. Your sister knows, though..." Confusion lingered as she went back and forth in her mind.

Should she tell him? But who would it benefit? She'd feel better having let go of her burden, but he could be endangered. Although Betsy was missing, possibly gone forever, they didn't know where she was—she might be looking for Charmaine at that very moment. And Buck was still on the island. Not to mention Frank. There was no telling who in Betsy's circle was in on her schemes.

She decided to tell him everything. She told Bradford about the jewellery, what Finn had said, and how she'd stumbled across it after her mother died. How she'd stowed it at the bank when she discovered Sean was looking for it, and how he wasn't going to stop coming after her until she gave it to him. But now that the police knew about it, they'd most likely ask her to hand it over. And then there was the small issue of Betsy or Buck breaking into her grandparents' house repeatedly over the years in an attempt to get the pieces back.

"Does Betsy know you're Charmaine Hilton?"

"Not that I'm aware of. She's always been lovely to me, treated me like a family member more than an employee. I know she's a murderer and that she is probably the one who chased my mother off the island when I was small, but I still can't believe she's such a monster. Maybe Bea was wrong." Tears pooled in the corners of her eyes. She had to pull herself together. She couldn't miss someone who had probably only pulled her close because she knew Charmaine had the jewellery and wanted to get her hands on it.

"I'm sorry, baby," Bradford said.

He wrapped his arms around her and held her close.

She sighed into his shirt. "The thing is, if she knew I had the jewellery, she could've taken it at any time. I had it hidden in my flat above her florist shop for months, and she had the key. But I never saw any sign that someone had searched the place. No, I don't think she knows who I am." Charmaine yawned again, this time the yawn seemed interminable.

"You go back to bed," Bradford said. "I'll sleep in the spare room. If you need me, tap on the wall or call out. I'm a light sleeper."

"Okay," she said. "Thanks for staying."

"Anytime," he replied.

She turned to walk back to her bedroom when he stopped her with a single word.

"Wait..."

Slowly, she turned to face him.

"I wanted to say this earlier at the office, but we were interrupted." He stepped towards her, closing the distance between them so that she could feel the warmth of his body. He laced his fingers through hers and kissed the back of her hand. "I'm glad we found each other."

"Me too."

"I had my heart broken a few years ago. My girlfriend, who I thought I'd spend my life with, told me she didn't love me and walked away. It was devastating. That on top of the way I lost Mum, and the destructive lifestyle I'd been leading for a long time. I didn't take it very well, and I hit rock bottom soon after."

She inhaled a quick breath. "I can understand that."

"I know you can. And the thing is, I went to counselling and I got healthy long before I met you. I wanted to find a way

117

to live a fulfilling life even if I never met anyone else to share it with. I had to let go of the idea that another person was the key to my happiness. But then you came along."

She grinned, her vision blurred with tears.

"You're so gentle and kind. You never force me to be someone I'm not or want to change me. You take everyone exactly as they are, accept them, and love them. I know we haven't been dating long, but I wanted to tell you how happy you make me. It's been a long time since I've felt so good."

She swallowed and wiped the tears from her eyes with her fingertips. "You make me happy too."

Seventeen

EVER SINCE HER conversation with Mum in the backyard by the pool, Taya had felt like a different person. The guilt that had eaten her up over not spending enough time with her parents, her years of rebelliousness towards them, had been forgiven and forgotten. She could finally move forward. She hadn't cried once since that afternoon, and she didn't feel the need. When she thought about her father, there was a deep sadness that still lingered in her heart, but it wasn't the gut-wrenching pain it'd been during the first weeks after losing him.

She reached into the boot of her car and pulled out armfuls of bags with decorations in them. Then she carried them to Penny's beach house and knocked on the door with her wrist.

"Come in!" Penny called.

Rowan opened the door as Taya was about to set the bags down to do it herself. He kissed her cheek and offered to get the rest of the things from the car.

"Thank you, Rowan. You're a gem."

Inside, she found Penny fussing about in the kitchen with

bags of chips and salsa plus a dozen bottles of soft drink on a table set with a white tablecloth.

"You didn't have to do that," Taya admonished her as she set down the bags on the bench top. She gave Penny a hug, awkwardly avoiding her enormous stomach. "I told you I'd take care of everything."

"I had to do something," Penny replied. "I've been lying around the house like a beached whale. Rowan's been very attentive."

They spent the next hour decorating Penny's beach house. Taya hadn't laughed as much in months as she did during that hour. She'd missed Penny's sweet nature, her feisty spirit, and her sense of humour more than she imagined. She hadn't noticed that her laughter was so muted while Penny was gone until now, when she finally laughed so heartily that it brought tears to her eyes. But thankfully, these tears were happy ones.

The guests began to arrive soon after, and the fun began. There were games to discover how big Penny's stomach was or what disgusting concoction of chocolate or Vegemite was which type of baby poop. Vegemite or Nutella as baby poop was a common baby shower game, one Taya had never appreciated in her twenties but now brought her to the verge of tears while she laughed at the various faces each of the women pulled as they tasted the contents of the disposable nappies. There were funny prizes and heartwarming speeches, and plenty of delicious food brought by Beatrice.

Charmaine was there taking photographs. Evie had offered, but Taya wanted her to relax and enjoy herself. Besides, Charmaine preferred to be behind a camera in a large crowd, she'd said. So, Taya gratefully accepted her offer. She looked a little pale, which she said was the result of a too much work and not enough food. Taya made her promise to take eat plenty at the party. She'd laughed at that, said "Yes, Mum," and trundled off to get her camera from the car.

When Penny's brother, Rob, showed up, he brought his wife and son with him. Taya hadn't seen his family in years, not since Julian was a baby. Jacqui looked older and had blonde highlights in her brunette curls. She seemed happy, and Taya was glad they were all together. She knew how much Rob longed for reconciliation.

"You look good," she said to Rob as they gathered around the food table, paper plates in hand.

"Thanks," he replied with a grin. "You too. I was sorry to hear about your dad."

She felt the familiar drop of her heart into her gut, but she ignored the emotion to focus on Rob. "Thank you. It was a shock to all of us, but we're learning to cope. I'm glad to see Jacqui and Julian here."

He turned to look at his family, his gaze wistful. "It's been a long time coming. She's agreed to give me another chance, and this time, I'm not going to blow it."

"Good for you," Taya said.

"One of the main reasons we split up is because I was gone so much with work. I wasn't there for her like I should've been, and she had a hard time with being a new mum. I didn't understand it at the time. I knew she was struggling, but I was too. I didn't know how bad it'd gotten until it was too late. She moved out and took Julian with her. She needed someone to help, so she went to live with her parents and said she didn't want to be married anymore. It broke my heart."

"I'm so sorry you went through that," Taya said. "But hopefully you can start fresh."

"Yes, I hope so too. I've decided that being a construction worker on major projects, always travelling around the state, isn't the best career for a family man. So, I've quit my job and bought a small construction company here on Coral Island." His eyes sparkled, and he tapped his nose with one finger. "But don't say anything yet. I want to surprise Penny."

"That's amazing," Taya said in a hushed voice. "She's going to be so happy, especially with the baby coming. They'll be cousins."

He shook his head slowly. "I never thought Julian would have a cousin on my side of the family. I'm over the moon about it."

"It is incredible. Penny and Rowan will be amazing parents."

Rob's smile faded. "Yeah, I hope so. But he's going to be away, going to miss so much of his child's life, like I did. I don't want to tell him off because it's his life, but if I could do it over again, I'd be there for it all — the everyday, mundane things. Not only the big stuff. It's the consistency, being available day after day, that builds the relationship. I've learned that the hard way. Julian barely knew me for years, but now we have a good connection. I'm hoping to build an even better one when we move back to Coral Island. I can teach him to fish, to dive, to gather oysters. I'm looking forward to it. I'm sick and tired of living inland where there's barely any rain, too much dirt, and no ocean. The island is home for me, and now it will be home for Julian too."

"Welcome home," Taya replied, giving Rob a hug. "I'm so glad you're back."

* * *

After the party was over, Taya and Penny collapsed into chairs on the back deck of the beach house. The view out over the water was spectacular. The moon had risen until it hung above the horizon. A bluish glow lit up the water, which sparkled and shone in an eerie reminder of how deep, dark and unknown it was.

"Thank you for the lovely party," Penny said with a sigh as she rubbed her neck with her fingertips.

"You're welcome, sweetie. It was my pleasure. I've always wanted to throw you a baby shower, by the way. I've been waiting a long time."

Penny laughed. "Can you believe it? Your daughter is in her twenties, and my child is yet to be born. They're not even close to being in the same generation."

"It's strange. I'm hoping to be a grandmother soon."

"Everyone will think I'm a grandmother," Penny replied with a pensive tone.

Taya playfully slapped her leg. "Don't worry about what anyone thinks. That's the beauty of being in your forties— you don't care anymore about what people say. It's your life —you live it how you want to, and I know you're going to love being a mum. I didn't get to appreciate it the way I would now. I was so stressed and anxious all the time, worrying about silly things like having a messy house or whether Camden was excelling at ballet. Things that didn't matter. When I lost Todd, my entire world came crashing down, but I still had to be a parent to Camden. I was on autopilot a lot. I sometimes wish I could go back in time and relish those moments with her — the cuddles in bed way before the sun rose, the sticky kisses, the messy playroom. So much of her childhood was me hurrying to clean up after her or to cook a meal before rushing off to the inn with her on my hip."

"You were a great mum, and you did the best you could," Penny said encouragingly.

"Yes, I was a good mum. And you will be too. But I was so stressed about so many things back then. Of course, I lost my husband and had a business to run. But I think I'd have a different outlook if I was starting out now. Don't worry about your age—think about how much more relaxed and at ease you're going to be with everything. You've already built your career, you know who you are, and you're capable and strong.

You can absorb and cherish every single moment with your child."

"Thanks, Taya. I appreciate that. It's so easy to feel over-whelmed sometimes."

"You are going to be fine. More than fine. You'll be great."

They sat in silence for a few minutes. Taya considered standing, but after a full day at work and then running around for three hours serving people and managing games at the party, she was completely exhausted. She let her eyes drift shut and almost fell asleep right there on Penny's porch. She startled and rose to her feet. "I should go before I pass out."

"Before you go, there was something I wanted to talk to you about."

Taya sat again, turned to face Penny, and blinked to keep herself awake. "I'm listening."

Penny sighed. "You know how Bea told us about Betsy being the murderer? I've been thinking about it a lot."

"That must've been a shock to you. I know you like Betsy."

Penny huffed. "More than a shock. I don't know what to say or do, how to process it. All my life, I've known Betsy Norton as the nice old lady at the flower shop. Now I find out she killed my grandmother? And the man I thought killed her is my father, and he's innocent. So, what does that mean? My mind is a complete jumble. I try to talk to Rowan about it, but he goes blank. I don't think he knows what to say. I'm not sure he even believes what Bea told us."

"That's understandable, I suppose. There's been so much speculation. And his entire life, he's seen Buck as the man responsible. The villain in his life's story."

"It's impacting him a lot more than he lets on," Penny whispered, glancing over her shoulder at the house to make sure Rowan wasn't nearby.

"I'm sorry, sweetie. I know that's hard on you."

"It is, but I'm also confused. Does this mean Buck isn't the bad guy? And if he's not the bad guy, should I give him a chance as my father and as a grandfather to our baby? I'm not sure I'm comfortable with that. After all, he did take advantage of my mother when she was a teen."

Taya pressed her lips together. It wasn't her place to tell Penny what to do, but she couldn't imagine trusting Buck, even if he was innocent of murder. Sometimes it was hard to let go of the past.

"You can tell me. I won't hold it against you," Penny said as if reading her thoughts.

"I don't trust him. I know he's apparently innocent, but I've thought he was a criminal for too long. Plus, that whole thing with your mother — it's disturbing."

"I know, but he's my dad."

"Maybe you can have a relationship with him, but let it form gradually and see how it goes."

"Maybe." Penny looked pensive. She stared out over the ocean, then grimaced. "I've got to go inside. My legs are getting stiff, and my back aches. I'm tired all the time."

"That's hard, I know. But as soon as the baby is out, you'll feel a lot better."

"Only six weeks to go!" Penny said, lumbering to her feet with Taya's arm for support.

"We should go shopping for baby things on the mainland."

"That would be fun, but I've been given an avalanche of gifts at this wonderful party. I'll go through everything and see if I still need a few items we can shop for."

Taya pouted. "I love shopping for babies. Let me spoil this little cutie pie. I don't care if you already have plenty."

"Fine, you can spoil him or her." She laughed. "You're going to be a wonderful auntie, Taya Eldridge."

"Auntie Taya. I like the sound of that."

Taya swatted at a mosquito on her leg, then they walked inside.

"I've been meaning to ask — would you be the baby's godmother?" Penny asked. She stopped and took Taya's hand, squeezing it gently. "It would mean the world to me."

Taya grinned. "I'd be honoured."

Eighteen

THE DAY of the reunion had snuck up on Bea. She wasn't ready for it. It felt like a mad rush and last-minute scramble to get everything ready for the event. Charmaine had been a big help. She had the list of RSVPs and had put together name tags for everyone. Bea had overseen decorations, and Charmaine had devised the scavenger hunt clues. It'd been fun pulling it all together, but Bea wasn't entirely convinced it would be a hit with the guests.

Plus, she was nervous about seeing people she hadn't spoken a word to in thirty years. Would she recognise anyone?

They were holding the reunion at the Blue Shoal Inn, but the scavenger hunt would take people all over Blue Shoal. It was the best venue for the event, and besides, it was Taya's establishment and so it held special meaning for the four friends. It was where they'd eaten their girls' lunches for the past few years, not to mention where Taya had lived, worked, and raised her daughter. Penny and Bea's weddings both included the inn, and Evie said she couldn't think of a better location. So, it was settled.

The dining room and adjoining rose garden had been

booked out for the evening, and they looked spectacular. There were twinkle lights everywhere. Bea had picked fresh greenery to decorate the tables, which were covered with white cloths. There were floral arrangements dotted throughout the venue, of course, thanks to Charmaine, and the delicious scents of roast beef, pork, and chicken wafted in the cool night air. A DJ was setting up in the corner and there were nineties movie posters hung on the walls.

"It looks fantastic," Charmaine said as she stuck a pen behind one ear. "You did a great job with the décor, Bea."

"Thank you. I'm happy with it. The guests will be here soon. Is everything ready to go?"

"All set," Charmaine said. "I've got my phone on me if you need anything."

"Are you sure the scavenger hunt isn't too cringe? You're young and hip. You can tell me, honestly."

Charmaine laughed. "Young and hip? Really? No, the hunt isn't cringe. It's adorably kitsch."

"Is that a good thing?"

"It'll be fun. I never thought I'd have to say this to anyone other than myself, but you need to lighten up." Charmaine arched an eyebrow.

Beatrice huffed. "I'm light."

"Uh-huh. I've got to go check people in. You okay here?"

"I'm great." Bea rubbed her hands together, then scanned the room for Aidan. She saw him over by the DJ.

"How does the music look?" she asked, coming up beside him.

"I'm helping pick out a playlist. I've requested all nineties songs, with a few from the eighties thrown in for good measure."

"That's perfect," she said. "Thank you."

"Are you feeling anxious?"

"A little. I'm not sure this was a good idea."

He placed his arms around her and held her close. "It's a great idea, and it looks wonderful. Everyone will have a good time, and we'll remember it forever."

"Thanks, honey." He always knew what to say to talk her down from the ledge.

Taya walked into the room looking even more stunning than she usually did. She wore a short chocolate-coloured dress and a simple gold necklace. Her shoes were azure, with thin straps and very high heels. She sported a matching azure clip in her sleek bob. She craned her neck, then her gaze found Bea and her stern expression morphed into a smile. She hurried to Bea and embraced her.

"You look amazing," Bea said. "Is this nineties? I don't know how you do it."

Taya glanced down at her dress as if surprised by it. "Do I? You look lovely too. I think this blue was popular then. Wasn't it?"

"I think you're right," Bea replied.

Bea had been happy when she looked in the mirror. She wore a simple navy one-shouldered dress, with a chunky silver necklace and matching silver pumps. Hers weren't high like Taya's. She'd never mastered teetering along in those impossibly high heels the way Taya had.

"Do you think that's Hairy Legs?" Taya asked, pointing across the room at a tall man with a shaved head wearing torn jeans and a plaid shirt.

Bea frowned. "Isn't he the guy who tried to get you to run off with him during high school?"

"That's him." Taya's face grew pink.

Bea studied the man. He looked so different — more mature, taller than she remembered, thicker build... and yet still familiar.

The room was filling up. She'd imagined this moment — as their old school friends congregated together — and it was finally happening. It was strange to see them after so much time. There were a number of faces she didn't recognise at all. She'd never thought she'd be able to forget a single one, but time had faded her recollections about so many things.

"It would be kind of romantic if he's still single," Bea said.

Taya huffed. "I'm not looking for a relationship. I've decided the solitary life suits me best."

"Oh, really?" Bea asked. "I'm sure you're right." There was no way that would last. Taya had been hurt by Andrew, but she'd also told Bea how good it was to have someone to spend time with, to attend the theatre with (something Taya loved to do), to share her life with. He hadn't been right for her, but someone would be. Bea only hoped Taya would open herself up to the opportunity of finding the right man someday, but she wasn't about to push her. Taya was stubborn. Pushing didn't do anything but prompt her to fight back.

"Excuse me. Are you Taya Eldridge?" The man approached and smiled at Taya and Bea.

Taya faced the man with wide eyes. "Hairy Legs?"

He laughed, his blue eyes twinkling. "No one has called me that in thirty years."

"Sorry. I meant to say, 'Hi, Brent. It's good to see you again.'"

"Would you like to dance?" he asked.

Taya glanced at Bea, her facial expression blank. But Bea could read between the lines. Taya was nervous but excited, although none of that showed on her face.

"Enjoy yourself!" Bea called after them as Brent led Taya to the small dance floor. Two other couples were there already, dancing to a compilation of nineties hits.

Aidan was looking for her. He caught her eye and made his way over to her, then offered her his hand. "Want to dance?"

Her heart skipped a beat. He was more handsome each

day. "I'd love to." She took his hand, and they walked together to the dance floor. Then he put his arms around her, and they swayed in time to the music. It was a slow number, and the music seemed to penetrate through to her very core. It was as if they'd travelled back in time and were in high school again. All around them were the people she'd spent those years with while the music they'd danced to swelled to fill the room.

Nineteen

DINNER WAS delicious and a lot of fun. Beatrice ran into people she didn't immediately recognise, but after they introduced themselves, the memories returned. There were conversations about families and marriages, careers, and life choices. Everyone seemed to be having a wonderful time—Taya especially, from what Bea could tell. Her place setting was close to Brent's, and the two of them were deep in conversation for much of the evening.

Finally, it was time for the scavenger hunt. Bea had purposely put herself, Taya, Evie, and Penny into a team for the game. The rest of the group was divided into four- or five-member teams as well.

Taya sidled up to Bea when she was ready to announce the hunt. "Can Brent join Aidan's team?"

"What? I've already put everyone into groups. And why don't you want him in ours?"

Taya's cheeks reddened. "It'd be good for him to spend time with the guys. And besides, we organised the whole thing. I think he'd have more fun with them."

"You don't want to spend more time together?"

"I don't know, I'm confused." Taya wrung her hands. "Can you do me this one favour? Brent's group has five. It doesn't matter if they lose one person."

Bea rolled her eyes. She could tell the entire evening would be this kind of compromise, but she couldn't say no to Taya, with her earnest face begging for help beneath the glow of the twinkle lights. "Fine, but don't tell anyone or they'll all want to change groups and we'll never get out of here."

"Thank you," Taya said, kissing Bea on the cheek before rushing off to tell Brent the news.

Bea walked between each of the groups, handing out the list of instructions and the first clue.

"Ready, set, go!"

The first challenge involved a style of bingo in which Bea called out names and people had to match faces on the sheet she'd given them. The first to match all the faces received the second clue. Most of the teams finished quickly and hurried to solve the clue.

Then, they ran off in the direction of the nearby beach. The second clue led them to the end of the beach, where a rock in the shape of an elephant squatted. Anyone who'd been to the beach in Blue Shoal knew it was there, so most of the competitors arrived at around the same time, puffing hard and laughing.

"We didn't think this through," Taya said, pulling her stilettos off with a grunt and peering at the sand-covered leather in dismay.

"I hope we don't give anyone a heart attack," Evie agreed as she shucked off her sandals too.

Penny had stayed behind at the top of the beach and waved to them from a distance.

"There's no way I'm running anywhere. But I'll drive if you need it," Penny had said with one hand on her belly before the rest of them leapt down to the sand to follow the group.

Bea removed her shoes as well and brushed the sand from them. Then she waited her turn to read the next clue. Charmaine had written the clues, and Beatrice had no idea where any of it would lead them. Her heart pounded against her ribcage — partly from the mad dash across the sand, and the rest was excitement. Aidan, Rowan, David, and Brent stood nearby.

Aidan shot her a wink. "You're going down, Bumble Bea."

She laughed. "Not a chance, Whitlock."

The clue was on a piece of cardboard. With black writing and gilded in gold, it was a poem about a fair maiden being captured by a dreaded pirate.

Bea tipped her head to one side and studied the cardboard. "How did Chaz come up with these challenges? I have no idea what this is."

"Let me see," Taya said.

"A pirate? On Coral Island?" Evie's nose wrinkled. "I should've paid more attention in history class. Of course, it was thirty years ago, so I don't remember a thing from that class other than the lesson that writing who you'll love forever on your folder won't make it so."

Bea laughed. "Very educational, then."

"I know what it is!" Taya shouted. Then she lowered her voice to a whisper. "The statue at the end of the pier. It's of a woman who was one of the early settlers. Her husband founded Blue Shoal. Remember, she disappeared and was never seen again? People said she was kidnapped from off the dock."

The three of them headed for the shore where Penny stood patiently waiting. The next two hours, each of the high school teams darted here and there all over, following clues — some cryptic, others simple. There were hoots of laughter, shrieks, shouts, and squeals emitted all over town. From what Bea could tell, everyone was having a fantastic time — learning about each other and the history of the Blue Shoal and the island. Some of the clues harked back to their high school years — like naming the valedictorian or the captain of the football team. Bea had fed Charmaine the details behind the answers, so she had the advantage at times, but she kept them to herself and let the others figure it out.

She savoured each moment, took photographs, and laughed out loud more times than she could count. It was far more fun than she'd thought it could be. There was even a mousse-eating challenge in the middle of the game that had everyone covered in chocolate and the entire town resounding with gales of laughter.

The final clue was a difficult one. Bea wasn't sure what Charmaine was thinking when she wrote it. It wasn't based on any of the information she'd given her. By this time, they'd driven all over Blue Shoal. Penny's car was small and cramped, and they'd been thrown against the windows more times than Bea could count as Penny careened around the tight corners in the small hamlet.

"Are you sure we're going in the right direction?" Taya asked from the front passenger seat as she held on to the handle above her head for dear life.

"What did the clue say again?" Evie asked.

Bea squeezed her eyes shut as she remembered. "'The road with the view; there are only two. Take the fork with the stork —you'll see what he can do." Bea's eyes blinked open.

"The only roads with a view are up here on the hill, so we're definitely headed in the right direction. As for the rest, I have no idea." Evie peered out the window into the darkness.

"We could be completely wrong," Bea said. "I haven't seen anyone else for at least ten minutes."

"We're either winning big or losing horribly," Taya replied with a giggle.

Bea hadn't seen Taya this happy in a long time. It was nice

to witness her almost giddy with excitement. She was her old self again, but with fewer inhibitions. Having the four of them back together was everything Bea had hoped for.

"Turn left," she said.

Penny slowed the car and turned. They were on a dark lane. Trees lined either side and blocked out the light of the moon. They crept along the road.

"I think this is the street with the best view," Taya said, squinting through the darkness.

"There's a stork!" Penny squealed.

They coasted past a painted metal bird next to a long driveway.

"We're going to win this for sure," Evie chirruped, clapping her hands together.

"I don't see any of the other groups," Bea added. "We could definitely win."

"Would that look bad, though?" Penny asked. "We did plan the entire reunion."

She had a point. Bea shrugged and continued staring out the window. "We have to find the clue. Let's worry about that when we find it."

Penny pulled the car over to the side of the road and parked. "I suppose we should get out and have a look around. But it sure is dark up here."

"This road looks familiar. These houses do too," Bea mused as she climbed out of the car and glanced around. "What street is it again?"

Penny huffed. "I don't know. I was trying not to crash. I didn't read the sign. But I did see the stork."

"Great work, honey," Taya said, patting her arm.

Penny laughed. "Thanks."

Evie jogged back to where the stork stood vigil beneath a streetlamp. "Here's the clue... It's taking us back to the inn. It's time for supper and dancing."

"Oh, thank goodness," Taya said. "I'm about to drop from exhaustion."

Bea laughed. "Me too. I'm too old to spend the entire night traipsing all over town. I had no idea we'd be doing so much running."

"And what about that rock climbing? I'm going to have a word with Charmaine when I see her," Taya replied. "She should've warned us to wear pants!"

Penny scanned the road one way, then the other. "Wait... Hey, I know where we are. This is Buck's street."

Evie was puffing lightly from her jog back to join them. "Oh, yeah. That's right. It is."

"Really?" Taya shivered, hugging herself.

"He's not a murderer anymore. I mean, he never was. I guess." Penny inhaled a quick breath. "It's all very confusing."

"Penny's right. There's no need to be afraid of him now that we know the truth," Bea said. "When we visited Buck before, he was nice to us. He's an old man who likes to garden and bake and whose sister killed someone fifty years ago. We can't hold that against him, can we? Plus, he's been investigated repeatedly, harassed, and then arrested for a crime he didn't commit. Maybe we should say hi. It can't hurt."

Taya and Evie exchanged a look. Taya nodded. "Sure, okay. Why not?"

Evie forced a smile. "I don't mind, if that's what you want to do. Do you have a torch in your car, Penny? I can't even see where to step."

"Sorry, I should add one to my glove box. I have them in my work trucks, but not this car."

"It's fine. We'll hold hands and walk slowly," Taya said, reaching for Penny. "The last thing we need is for you to trip on something and fall."

Bea took Evie's hand, and the four of them set off down

the street, walking slowly and watching carefully where they placed their feet.

"Do you think the others have already been here?"

"Definitely," Evie replied. "The cardboard with the clue was pretty tattered and lying on the ground next to the stork rather than in its beak, where there was some tape flapping about."

"Oh, darn. We're not going to win," Bea replied. "And the fact that we're the only ones here means we're probably last, then."

"Never mind," Taya said. "We'll head back in a minute and tear up the dance floor. We don't need a silly prize—we've got moves."

"It was a holiday in Airlie Beach," Bea replied.

"Yeah, we can go there any time we want on the ferry," Evie said in a defiant tone. "We don't need it."

"You're right," Bea said. "We've got each other."

"The Fabulous Four, back together again," Penny said.

They stopped outside Buck's house, and Penny knocked on his front door. The porch light was on, and a soft glow emitted through the curtains at the front window. The door opened, and Buck stood there in a pair of jeans and a shirt with a spatula in his hand.

"Hi," he said, offering a confused smile. "Everything okay?"

"Hello, Buck. It's Penny. Sorry to drop in unexpectedly like this, but we were in the neighbourhood, and I thought it might be nice to see you."

* * *

Taya, Bea, Penny, and Evie sat in chairs at Buck's dining room table while he chattered on about dinner plans and how there was plenty to go around if they were interested.

"I've been gardening all afternoon, and when I stopped, I fell asleep in my favourite armchair. So, I'm only now having dinner. Grilled cheese. Anyone else hungry?"

"No, thanks," Taya said.

"We've already eaten," Penny explained.

There was a thud in the next room. It startled Bea. She was on edge, sitting in Buck's kitchen. She'd heard Betsy confess to the murder with her own two ears, but something about Buck still unsettled her. She couldn't help it. The fear she'd felt around him was difficult to forget, even with the latest developments in the case.

"What was that?" she asked.

He glanced in the direction of the sound. "Nothing. So, what brings you to Blue Shoal?"

Sweat beaded on his forehead. Bea's eyes narrowed. Another thump made her fidget in her chair. "Do you own a cat?"

"What? No cats here." He laughed.

"We're having a high school reunion," Penny said. "We've got to get back. It's still going on."

"Well, don't let me stop you," he said. "If you have to go, you have to go."

He turned off the stove and moved to usher them in the direction of the front door. Bea stood with the others and walked awkwardly ahead of him.

"Uh, okay. I guess I'll see you another time."

He nodded, smiling. "It was nice of you to stop by."

Footsteps in the hallway, as though someone crept towards them, made Bea's heart thud. "Is there someone else in the house?"

"Of course not..."

Penny bustled past Buck and stepped into the hallway. "Betsy!"

Betsy strutted into the living room and regarded the group

through narrowed, dark eyes. "Hello, ladies. How lovely to see you all. I hope you didn't come all this way to pay me a visit." She laughed.

"Didn't Frank report you missing?" Taya asked.

Buck was pale. He lowered himself into an armchair. "Betsy stopped by. I don't know where she's been and she didn't give me any warning."

"He's as clueless as usual," Betsy added, waving a hand in his direction. "Some things never change."

"I thought you were on the run from the police," Penny said, her chin jutting out.

"I'm leaving tonight, but I've misplaced some jewellery that means a lot to me. You wouldn't happen to know where it is, would you?" She studied each of their faces one by one.

"Of course not," Taya huffed. "You must think you're so clever, fooling us for all these years. But we cared about you. We were your community, your friends. And you betrayed us."

Betsy shook her head. "You couldn't understand, honey. You've never been in an impossible situation like mine. I did what I had to do to protect my family, and I'd do it again in a heartbeat."

Penny's eyes flooded with tears. "You killed my grandmother. I thought you were my friend."

Betsy's cheeks grew red. "I didn't want to do it. But like I said, I didn't have a choice. She was threatening me. Said she'd turn Buck in for what he'd done. If she did that, I'd have lost everything. My husband would've found us. He'd have killed me and taken Frank."

"You could've gone to the police."

"Haven't you figured it out yet? The police on this island are hopeless. They wouldn't have done anything to protect me. And where could I go then?"

Just then, the sound of sirens drifted in on the evening

breeze. Betsy's eyes grew wide, and she hurried to the window to look out. Then her shoulders slumped.

"I'm too old to run. They'll be here in a minute." She turned to Buck, lifted his cheeks with her palms, and looked into his eyes. "I love ya, brother, even if you do drive me crazy sometimes. Take care of Frank and Sam for me."

When the police burst in, Betsy stood with her hands loose at her sides, her grey curls wild all over her head, and her pink silk kaftan flowing elegantly around her ankles.

The officer in charge read her rights as he arrested her, and they led her out to the police car. Another officer spoke to the group.

"Stay where you are. We're going to need statements from all of you."

Twenty

WHEN THEY FINALLY MADE IT back to the reunion, most of the guests had left. There were a few intoxicated couples moving slowly to the music on the dance floor. The men were seated at the bar, talking and laughing over drinks. Charmaine watched the four ladies hobble into the room with horror. She'd been frantically searching for and calling the group for the past two hours. She'd started to believe they'd fallen into the ocean or had a car accident or something equally distressing.

Taya, Evie, Bea, and Penny had bare feet and were dishevelled, sweaty, and exhausted. They fell one by one into chairs. Charmaine walked over to meet them, her brow furrowed.

"I'm so thirsty," Bea said.

Charmaine scanned their faces. "What on earth? Where have you been? Everyone else got back from the scavenger hunt hours ago. I was about to call search and rescue."

"We confronted a murderer..."

"And were almost arrested."

"I fell and twisted my ankle." Bea held out one foot and

pressed gingerly at the wounded joint. She'd tripped on a rock when they were walking back to the car in the dark.

"You poor things. I can't believe it. Everyone else had such a wonderful time, and you missed all the dancing." Charmaine glanced at the gyrating couples on the dance floor. "Well, almost all of it."

"I don't think I could dance a step anyway," Taya said, wriggling her toes.

"The police will be here any moment to finish taking our statements," Bea said.

Charmaine's frown deepened. "What happened out there? And why were you almost arrested? Did you do something dangerous?"

Penny began to giggle. She laughed so hard her belly shook, which triggered the other ladies to burst into laughter as well. Charmaine watched on in confusion. Had they experienced some kind of communal psychotic episode? They'd all cracked at once. Perhaps this was what happened when friends became as close as they were.

Finally, Penny wiped her eyes and stopped laughing. "We did something stupid. We went to see my father."

"Buck Clements? Oh, dear," Charmaine said, setting her clipboard down and dropping into a chair beside Penny.

"Then we found Betsy in his hallway," Bea added.

"And the police showed up and arrested her," Evie finished.

Charmaine pressed both hands to her forehead. "Betsy's still on the island?"

"Yep. But now she's at the police station. We can finally all relax."

"But why are the police coming to see you?" Charmaine asked.

"We had to make statements, but we ran out of time. They

said they'd meet us here to finish up. They should be here any moment."

The men sauntered over from the bar. David wound an arm around Evie's waist. Aidan greeted Bea with a kiss, then studied her, concern etched across his features. "Are you okay? Where have you been?"

Each of the ladies explained her whereabouts to the men while Charmaine hurried over to the bar to pay the staff and the DJ and to give him a ten-minute warning. The reunion was over and it'd been a raging success, apart from having the organisers disappear midway through. At least they were back now. Charmaine had hidden how frantic she'd felt inside over their disappearance. She'd called each of their phones a dozen times while smiling at the rest of the guests and handing out prizes. She was more than grateful that it was all over, and everyone was back safe and sound. She couldn't wait to fall into bed in her cosy little beach cottage.

A voice behind her made her heart go cold. "It's nice to see you, sis. You look good."

She spun around to find herself face-to-face with Sean. Her brother suited the spiky hair and the well-cut suit he wore. He looked handsome and debonair, his half smile making him appear mischievous when she knew it went further than that. He was cold and calculating.

"What do you want, Sean?"

"That's not a very polite way to greet your brother, Chaz. Especially when I haven't seen you in months."

"I'm sorry — how are you? Fine weather we've been having. I hope you enjoyed your ferry ride over to the island. Now, what are you doing here? We had an agreement."

His grin widened. "That's much better. And yes, I'm enjoying the weather. There's no place like Coral Island. I see you moved. When I broke into the flat, there was no one there. Not even that ugly cat you liked to fawn over. Where do you live now, sis? A brother should know where his sister stays, don't you think? I thought I might follow you home, but instead you came here. Seems like you never stop working. That's an affliction I don't share."

"I'm going to ask you one more time, and then you need to leave. I paid you to stay away from Coral Island. So, why did you come back? What do you want?"

"You know what I want, sis."

"But I already gave you money."

"I don't want your money. I want the jewellery. I know you have it. I've searched the house—I've asked around at the bank in Newcastle. No one knows anything about any jewellery. Not the accountant, or the solicitor, none of Mum's friends. So, the only logical explanation is that you have it. I'll admit, you did a good impression of a clueless person the last time I was here. You even had me convinced. But now I want my jewellery. And I want it now." His smile disappeared, and his face turned thunderous. "Hand it over."

"Everything okay here?" Aidan asked, stepping in between Charmaine and Sean.

Sean's smile reappeared as quickly as it had gone. "All good, it's a family reunion. Right, sis?"

Charmaine didn't want Aidan to get in the middle. This was her fight and hers alone. No one else should be hurt because of her family or the drama that'd surrounded them for so many years, she couldn't remember how it felt to live without it. "We're okay. Thanks, Aidan. Sean is leaving."

"I think I'll stay until you give me what I came here for." He stepped closer, his looming presence menacing.

The staff were packing up the restaurant and dance floor around her. Guests were being encouraged to find their things and leave. Charmaine couldn't move. She was frozen in place. If she moved, Sean might do something they'd both regret. All the people left in the room were her friends. She couldn't stand for any more of them to be harmed by her brother.

"It's at the bank," she said. "I can't get it now—the bank's closed."

"You brought it here? I should've known. I tried asking at the bank in town, but they wouldn't cooperate. I guess they like you better than they do me. I guess we can head home for a good night's sleep then, and we'll go to the bank together in the morning."

"I think you should go," Aidan said, taking another step towards Sean. Evie's boyfriend, David, came into view, a frown on his face. He didn't understand what was happening, but seemed ready to intervene if necessary. Charmaine didn't want anyone to get hurt. Her brother was so unpredictable. All of this was her fault, she shouldn't have come.

Sean's eyes narrowed. "You're a bit overconfident there, Grandpa."

Charmaine pressed a hand to her mouth. She wanted to scream, to shout, to say something, anything to make it stop.

Aidan shook his head and laughed. "Why don't you leave your sister alone, Sean? We can discuss it more tomorrow."

Sean lunged, his fist aiming directly at Aidan's nose. Aidan caught his hand firmly, twisted it up until it was behind Sean's back, and within moments had Sean hopping on tiptoe, yelping with pain. David helped Aiden to hold Sean still.

Charmaine strode around the two of them to stand directly in Sean's line of sight. "I guess you didn't remember that Aidan was a professional football player for years. Not very bright to try punching a footballer, is it, Sean?"

Aidan offered her a wink, prodded Sean in the direction of the bar. Just then, the police wandered into the restaurant. They saw Aidan with Sean and hurried to intervene, soon placing Sean under arrest. They left with him shouting for Charmaine to help bail him out. She ignored him and went to sit with her friends. They'd ordered her a drink, and they all sat in a circle outside on the deck with the sounds of the ocean in the distance and mused over the events of the evening.

"I'm glad you're okay," Bea said. "I sent Aidan over to help you, but the rest of us kept our distance. We weren't sure what to do."

"You did the right thing," Charmaine replied. "I don't want any of you to get hurt because of me. You've been through enough. The police have him now, and I'm sure they'll be able to determine that he was the arsonist who burned down your café and bookshop. I'm so sorry about all of it. I feel terrible."

"Never mind," Bea said. "We both got insurance payouts and have moved on to other adventures. The main thing is, you're safe. We're all safe."

"I'll drink to that," David said, raising his glass high. He clinked his drink against Evie's, and the rest of the group followed suit. They drank together, and Charmaine felt the weight of fear and doubt, of loss and regret, lift from her shoulders. Sean was finally locked away—Betsy too. Perhaps now they could all get back to some semblance of a normal life together on Coral Island.

Twenty-One

TWO MONTHS LATER, Charmaine was working in the florist shop on her own. She'd hired three high school students to help her out on afternoons and weekends. But most of the time, she was in the shop alone. It was Betsy's business, but with Betsy in prison, she wasn't sure what to do with it. Should she keep managing it until told otherwise? Surely Betsy would reach out to her at some stage to give her some direction. She couldn't simply abandon it. Besides, she'd never get paid that way. Betsy must have set up the payroll to continue automatically, so she received a paycheck every two weeks. If she stopped working, she couldn't keep collecting that.

So, she continued working, serving customers, and delivering flowers to weddings and events all over the island. There was a sadness to her days, though, thinking about her boss in prison, the murderer who'd gotten away with it for fifty years but was also the only mother figure she had left in this world.

It was confusing, concurrently loving and despising someone who'd had such an impact on her life in so many ways.

She'd set up her paints and easel in the back of the shop so she could watch for customers during the day while painting in her downtime. It wasn't the kind of business that stayed hectic all day long. There were stretches of quiet, and this gave her a chance to add to the collection of paintings hanging on the shop walls.

She swept up a pile of leaves near the doorway and then scooped them into the rubbish bin. When she returned to her painting, she held the brush poised over the seascape for several long minutes before drawing the brush down the side of the canvas to add texture to the waves.

An art dealer had stopped by the shop yesterday to ask her about the artists who exhibited there — he'd heard good things, he said.

"Do they have representation?"

She'd said she didn't think so. Would he like to speak to Finn Hilton?

"Yes, and Charmaine Billings. They're both very talented. I'd like to put together a showing in Cairns."

So, she'd set up a meeting with herself and Finn and the art dealer that afternoon, and they'd signed a contract for a showing six months from the date. Butterflies flapped in her gut as she thought about it. She needed to finish two dozen paintings before then; she wasn't sure how she'd manage it. It was exciting and scary — putting something out there that reflected a piece of herself for everyone to study, criticise, reject. Her instinct was to pull back, to say no, to run. But she held herself together, nodded sagely, and shook the man's hand when he left. Then she and Finn had squealed, hugged each other, and danced to a song on the radio with the sound turned up.

The bell over the front door jangled, and Charmaine looked up in surprise to see Frank and Samantha walk in.

Sam ran to Charmaine and threw her arms around Charmaine's waist.

"Sam! I haven't seen you in an age." Charmaine's eyes filled with tears as the girl squeezed her hard. "I missed you."

Sam took a step back, her mood somber. "We're moving."

"You are?" Charmaine looked up to see what Frank would say about that.

He nodded. "Yep. All packed and ready to go." He waved a hand towards the road behind him. There was a small moving truck parked at the curb.

"Where are you going?"

Frank stepped closer and handed Charmaine a piece of paper. It was wrinkled and covered in text. She glanced at it then back to him, her brow furrowed. "What's going on, Frank?"

"I'm sorry, Chaz. I have some bad news."

Her stomach tightened. She was being thrown out. She'd have to leave the florist's. If she didn't find a job, maybe she'd have to abandon the island and the life she'd built entirely. It wasn't fair—she'd finally found happiness. "Okay..."

"Betsy died."

His words were like a punch to the gut. She gasped, the wind knocked from her lungs. She hadn't expected that. She thought he'd talk to her about the shop or the flat, or money, or something else. Anything other than that.

"She died? How?" Her eyes flooded with tears against her will. She didn't want to cry in front of him—it was silly. He was Betsy's son. Betsy was a murderer. Why was she crying?

He looked at her kindly. "She had a heart attack in jail. I'm sorry. I know you cared about her."

She pressed a hand to her mouth to stifle a sob. "Thank you for telling me. And I'm sorry for your loss."

She glanced at Sam, who was watching her with wide,

reddened eyes. Charmaine held her arms open, and Sam fell into them, sobbing against her shirt.

"Oh, honey, I'm so sorry," she said, rubbing a circle on Sam's back.

Tears wound down Charmaine's cheeks. She gave up trying to keep them at bay. It was no use, not with Sam's face buried into her side, her tears soaking through the fabric.

Frank walked into the back of the shop, leaving the two of them alone. He returned a few moments later with a box beneath his arm. "Mum's coin collection and some photographs." He patted the box. "Plus a few sentimental trinkets. I'm leaving the rest. You can have it."

"What?" she asked, wiping her nose with the back of her hand and scanning the register for the tissue box. "No, you should take it all."

He shook his head. "That paper I gave you is a photocopy of the will. She left you the shop and everything in it. The flat as well. It's all yours."

Charmaine gaped and glanced around the building, taking it all in. This made no sense. She wasn't a relative. Frank and Sam needed it more than she did.

"But what about you and Sam?"

"She left us more than we'll ever need," he replied. "It seems my mother had socked away a real estate portfolio that I knew nothing about. Don't worry about us."

Sam released Charmaine and rubbed her wet cheeks with her hands. "I wish you'd come with us."

"Sorry, sweetie. I can't do that. But I'll visit. Where will you be?"

"We're going to see Mum."

Charmaine arched an eyebrow and met Frank's gaze. "Really?"

His cheeks pinked. "She's giving us another chance. I told her that we missed her and that my mother died, and she said she'd missed us too and asked us to come and live with her. We're going to be a family again."

"I'm so happy for you. That's the best news I've heard in months."

He grinned. "Thanks. If you're ever in Sydney, look us up. Okay?"

"I will."

She waved goodbye when they left, then stood in the middle of the shop and looked around. Her tears dried, and she drew a deep breath. The shop was hers. It was all hers. She couldn't believe it. She'd never imagined she would have anything so beautiful all to herself.

Twenty-Two

"IT'S TOO cold to sit outside," Beatrice said as she stepped through the glass sliding door from the porch and back into the house.

"You've definitely lived too long on Coral Island if you think this is cold," Penny replied, waving a hand in front of her face. "I'm hot."

"You're always hot," Bea replied with a laugh. "You're nine months pregnant."

"And my ankles are cankles." Penny crossed her eyes. "I'm enormous."

"I think you're retaining a bit of water, so that will go as soon as you have the baby."

"I hope so. I can't believe how much bigger I am."

"You'll be fine," Bea replied, although she was a little concerned at how puffy her friend's face had become. She knew from the experience of several of her friends back in Sydney that it might signal preeclampsia, and hoped Penny would be okay.

"How can I help with dinner?" Penny asked, sliding onto the couch and raising her feet on the footrest.

"You can sit there and sip on a lovely mocktail. I've got it covered." Bea returned to the open kitchen, where platters of antipasto waited on the bench and a pan of enchiladas heated in the oven. "I hope Buck likes Mexican food because that's what we're having. Enchiladas with Mexican rice, refried beans, and a fresh salad. Plus margaritas, of course." She poured a cocktail mixture from a glass jug into a cup and brought it to Penny. "Yours are virgin. Don't mix the glass jug with the porcelain one, since it has the hard stuff in it."

"Glass not porcelain. Got it." Penny took the drink and sipped. "Delicious, thank you. You're the best friend a girl could have, Bea. I don't know how I would've done this without you. I'm exhausted all the time. Rowan is busy working; he's supposed to be here by now, but he's late to everything when he's on a deadline. And I'm nervous about seeing Buck again."

"I'm happy to do it. You know how much I love to entertain. Besides, I get it — I'm nervous to see Buck as well, and he's not my biological father."

"How is this going to work?" Penny asked. "I say, 'hey, Dad, it's nice to see you even though your sister killed my grandmother because you knocked up my teenaged mother. Want to come to Christmas dinner with the family?'"

Bea almost choked on an olive. She coughed it up into a napkin, laughing. "Stop it, you nearly killed me."

"Sorry. But I'm serious — I don't know how to handle this. I need some advice."

"I think you need to take it slow. We'll have dinner tonight, and don't put any pressure on yourself for more than that. Think of it as a *sorry we all thought you were a murderer and told the police to arrest you* dinner."

"Maybe you're right."

"Let's see how it goes. After that, if you ever choose to see him again, it will be up to you. But I doubt you'll be besties wearing matching PJs to brunch anytime soon."

The doorbell rang. Bea went to open it and found Rowan holding a bunch of colourful flowers. He handed them to Bea and kissed her cheek. "Thanks for doing this for us."

"You're very welcome. Come on in, Penny's in the living room. Would you like a drink?"

Aidan jogged downstairs fresh from the shower and fixed a drink for himself and Rowan, while Bea finished up in the kitchen. Then the doorbell rang again.

Bea and Penny exchanged a nervous glance. It was going to be okay. Surely?

Aidan went to the door and brought Buck back with him. The older man had combed his grey hair neatly and wore a buttoned shirt with a pair of slacks. He glanced around the room, taking in everyone's faces.

"Hi," he said. "Thanks for having me. Don't worry, I promise not to kill anyone."

The tension broke and they all laughed together, even Rowan, which Bea was glad to see. Rowan had seemed so tense over the whole idea of Buck's visit.

"Come on in and take a seat, Buck. Can I get you something to drink?" Bea asked.

He requested a beer and sat beside Penny. They immediately dove into small talk, while Bea opened the beer and carried it over to Buck, who thanked her. She didn't want to pry, but she was curious to know what they were talking about.

"... won't be working at the refuge for a while, with this little one coming."

He glanced at her stomach as though seeing it for the first time. "I hadn't heard you were expecting."

"Any day now."

"Congratulations."

"Thank you."

"I didn't get to raise any of my own children." His face reddened. "As you know. You were my only biological child. Although I got to help raise Rowan, so that was ... well, one of my proudest achievements, even if I didn't do much."

The entire room fell silent. Rowan stared at his own feet. Penny cleared her throat. Bea wrung her hands together. "I'll bring the appetiser plates in. I hope you're all hungry."

She hurried back to the kitchen, and Aidan followed her.

"What are you doing?" she hissed, shooing him away.

"I'm helping you with the food," he replied, perplexed.

"Didn't you hear what's going on in there? It's a train wreck waiting to happen. They need you out there to interject if anything goes wrong. Our only job is to make sure no one yells at anyone else. If we can get through the night without that happening, I'll be ecstatic."

"I don't know how I'm supposed to stop people from yelling. I've never managed to stop you." He huffed.

She laughed and shook her head. "Off you go."

"Not fair you get to hide in the kitchen," he said as he wandered back to the living room.

Bea soon returned with two platters. They were heavy, and she wished she'd let Aidan help her, but she made it there without dropping them. By the time she sat down, the entire group was engaged in pleasant conversation and her anxiety eased.

They made it through the appetisers, then Bea and Aidan served the main course. The enchiladas were delicious; Bea had an old recipe she'd used for decades. It was one of her faithful favourites. Wherever she served it, people loved it.

There were more margaritas to go around, and the conversation had become easier. At that moment, Penny gasped. She set her glass down on the table, and slid her chair back, then stared at the floor.

"What is it?" Bea asked, jumping to her feet. "A spider? I'll get the broom."

"No, not a spider. My water broke." Penny's face went pale.

Bea grinned. "Well, how about that? Here comes the baby."

* * *

The first time they called the maternity ward at the local hospital, they were told to wait until contractions were five minutes apart before heading in. So, Bea helped to clean up the water and found Penny a change of clothes. Then they all retired to the living room to eat dessert on their laps and play a game of Monopoly.

Penny said it would help get her mind off the occasional contraction and the impending birth. They had a great time. It turned out that Buck was quite the businessman when it came to fake money and pretend properties and soon became a real estate tycoon collecting exorbitant rent from the rest of them.

Penny couldn't concentrate so continued to forget to roll the dice, or which character was hers, and where she was supposed to be. Rowan jumped in to help her and massaged her lower back when she needed it.

Bea couldn't focus either; she was worried about Penny. The labour would be riskier due to her age, and she knew how hard labour could be at the best of times. Was Penny ready for what she was about to experience? Bea had gifted her the book *Up the Duff* at her baby shower, which was the funniest pregnancy book she'd ever read, and so she should at least know a few things about what to expect. Still, no one was ever quite ready for labour when it happened the first time.

"Another contraction," Penny said.

Bea looked at her watch. "That's five minutes."

Rowan met Penny's gaze. "I guess that means we're off. We have your baby bag in the car. We're ready. Aren't we?"

Penny nodded. "I think so. Bea? What do we need?"

"I checked your bag already, remember? You've got everything you need. The main thing is that you and Rowan are both there. I can bring you anything else when the time comes."

"Right, okay. Thanks. Let's go then." Penny looked panicked.

"You'll be fine, Pen. It's going to be wonderful."

Rowan helped Penny to her feet. "Will you come too?" Her pleading look melted Bea's heart.

"Of course, we'll follow in our car. Right, honey?"

Aidan nodded. "Yes, if you'd like us to."

"Please," Penny said. "And, Buck, could you drive us? I know it's a lot to ask. But I'd like Rowan to sit with me."

Buck's eyes gleamed. "Absolutely. I'm happy to."

They all trundled out to the garage and driveway. Bea and Aidan climbed into Aidan's truck, while Penny, Buck, and Rowan got into their car. Aidan backed down the driveway and followed them to the hospital. All the while, Bea chewed on a fingernail.

"Do you think she's okay?" she asked.

"Why wouldn't she be?"

"I don't know. I'm worried for some reason."

"I'm sure she's fine. Shouldn't you let Taya and Evie know what's going on? I wonder if Penny has thought to call her family?"

"Good thinking," Bea said. She made a few quick phone calls. First to Penny's mother, who had no idea her daughter had gone into labour. Then she called Taya who squealed in delight and promised to be at the hospital as soon as she could manage it, but she was in the middle of a run. Then, Evie's went to voicemail. No doubt she was still working. The new job had been taking up a lot of her time lately, which Bea was thrilled about for both Evie and Bradford.

They pulled into the parking lot at the hospital, then helped Penny into the building. Buck followed at a distance, seeming unsure of what to do. When they took a seat in the waiting room, Rowan walked over to Buck.

"Thanks for driving us, Buck. I appreciate it. Can I give you money for an Uber home?"

Buck waved him off. "No need for that. I might stay a while if you don't mind. These things can take an age, but if it doesn't bother you, it would be nice to know she made it through."

Rowan looked surprised. "That's fine. I'll make sure to let you know how it goes. Thanks again."

They took Penny back to the labour ward quickly since her contractions continued to escalate. And within two hours, Rowan came out to the waiting room to announce that they'd had a healthy baby girl called Isla Penelope and showed them all a photo. By that time, both Taya and Evie had arrived. Penny's parents were on their way but hadn't made it yet from the mainland. The entire party jumped up and down and cheered, hugged Rowan and each other. Buck stood to one side, beaming. Rowan walked over to him and gave him a quick hug, which made Buck's eyes glisten.

"She's not seeing visitors yet," Rowan said. "But maybe in a few days. Thanks for coming."

Bea and Aidan walked back to his truck, his arm slung around her shoulders. She felt as though she'd run a marathon.

"I'm exhausted, and I didn't even give birth. I don't know how she's going to do this."

"It's a lot," Aidan admitted. "I can't say I know what it's like to have a baby, but I'm happy for them."

Bea patted his chest gently with her hand. "I know you wish you could've been there when Grace was born."

He nodded, his brow furrowed. "More than anything. But I can't go back in time."

"We'll have to be the loving aunt and uncle for Isla."

"I can live with that." He kissed the tip of her nose and opened the truck door for her.

She slid onto the seat and leaned her head back against the rest.

"Home?"

She opened her eyes. "Yes, please. I need sleep."

"We can clean up the kitchen tomorrow."

"I like you better all the time," she replied, reaching for his hand and winding her fingers through his.

"Back atcha," he said.

Twenty-Three

THE BEACH COTTAGE was lit up with lamps in every room and tiki torches out along the narrow path that led down to the beach. Charmaine peered out the window then nodded in satisfaction. This would be the first dinner party she'd ever thrown. She was so nervous her stomach was in a twist. But she had no time to wallow in introverted self-pity over having put herself into this situation, since her guests would be there any moment.

She set the table with placemats, silverware, and china. Bea had left some of her things behind at the cottage for Charmaine to use. She said she didn't need them once she moved in with Aidan. Which was perfect for Charmaine, who owned virtually nothing.

It'd been two weeks since Penny and Rowan had their baby. They wouldn't be coming to the dinner party as they weren't ready to leave the house yet. That's what Penny had whispered into the phone when Charmaine called. Then the baby had cried, and Penny had sworn beneath her breath and said, "I've got to remember to turn off the ringer on my phone." And then she hung up.

Charmaine had stared at the phone for a few seconds in surprise. She'd have to text Penny in the future. She hadn't even thought about waking the baby. It was funny how quickly she'd forgotten so much of what it was like to be a new mother. Hopefully Penny wasn't too upset with her.

Never mind, she'd thought to herself, Bea and Aidan, Evie and David were all coming. Taya was on a work trip, so she wouldn't be there either. But Bradford was on his way — he hadn't been able to get away from work any earlier or he would've helped, he assured her. But she wasn't concerned, it'd been fun to pull the dinner party together on her own. She'd used recipes from the internet and had tidied the house until it sparkled. She was ready.

Bradford was the first to arrive. He strode in carrying a box filled with soft drinks, wine, and beer and set it down on the kitchen bench. Charmaine hurried to kiss him, then helped him stack the drinks in the fridge.

"How was work?"

"It was good. Busy," he said. "Evie is such a gem. I'm glad I asked her to open the office here on the island. She barely needs any oversight now that she's learned how things work. It goes to show that employing someone with small business experience is worth it — they're used to having to figure everything out on their own. There's no one else to ask if you're not sure about something, you have to get it done. And she's doing that."

"That's great," Charmaine replied. "I know Evie was worried about what she'd do without the bookshop."

"She told me she's happier than she's been in a long time, because we're already pulling in a profit, and she doesn't have constant anxiety over paying the bills."

"You're a good man," Charmaine replied, standing on tiptoe to kiss him again.

He wrapped his arms around her and pulled her close to

deepen the kiss. He was everything she'd always wished she could find in a man and more. She felt so safe and loved when he held her that way.

"How did it go with the police? Didn't you meet with them today?" Bradford asked.

Charmaine was putting together a fresh salad. She sliced a red capsicum. "It was fine. They took photographs of the jewellery and sent it off to the USA. Apparently, it was stolen in some big heist over fifty years ago. They're shipping it back next week. It's worth millions."

"Wow, that's amazing."

"I know — it was a famous robbery. So, I've been holding onto jewellery from a famous robbery, and before that, Mum had it hidden in our house for years. It's so strange to think about."

"And did they ask you about Betsy's shop?"

"Yes, they were very interested in the fact that Betsy left me the shop. I could tell they were wondering if there was a connection between us that I hadn't told them. But I was honest with them, said it was a complete surprise, that Betsy and I were close, and I had no idea she was involved in Mary Brown's murder. They seemed to believe me. At least I hope they did. Thinking about it sets nerves jangling in my stomach."

"I still can't believe she did that, gave her shop to you."

"Me either," Charmaine replied. "But I'm excited about it. I've got all sorts of plans for how to expand it and grow the business. Now that it's mine, I want it to be a wedding and event planning enterprise as well as flowers."

"Will you change the name?" Bradford asked.

She frowned. "Hmmm... I don't think so. I still like Betsy's Florals."

"It *is* well known..."

"Infamous even," Charmaine quipped.

When Bea and Aidan arrived, they presented Charmaine with a delicious-looking pineapple upside-down cake with vanilla ice cream for dessert. She put the ice cream in the freezer and poured them each a glass of wine.

Then, Evie came with David. Charmaine had wondered how David would fit with the group the first time he'd come to one of their events, but since then, he'd proven himself to be a natural. He got along with everyone as though he'd always been there, and they welcomed him easily and warmly. Evie seemed happy and relaxed, more than she'd ever been since Charmaine had known her.

They wandered down to the beach with drinks in hand to take a short walk. The moon shone overhead, and stars twinkled across the dark canopy. The waves lapped quietly at the shore, and the sand was wet and cold underfoot.

Charmaine couldn't think of a time when she'd been more content. When she first arrived on Coral Island, she'd thought her life would never move beyond the point of survival. She'd spent three years fleeing from the overwhelming grief of losing her mother, never finding a place to call home, never settling down, never connecting with anyone. She'd struggled to pay her bills or even to speak to strangers. But now her time on the island had changed everything. She had a home, a business, a family, and friends.

Together they walked back to the house where Charmaine served lasagne and salad for dinner. They ate and talked, laughed, and reminisced.

"I still can't believe we ended up giving police statements at the reunion," Bea said, raising her glass in a toast. "Let's drink to never having to speak to the police again in our lives."

"I'll second that," Evie replied.

They all raised their glasses and drank.

"It's hard to believe they finally found Penny's grandmother's murderer," Aidan said.

"And it all started here," Evie added. "With Bea and her cottage."

"If you hadn't moved back here and renovated this cottage, none of us would ever have discovered the truth," Bradford said.

"The film canister started it all," Bea agreed.

"To Bea and her cottage," Charmaine said, raising her glass again.

They all cheered and toasted, then drank. Bea and Aidan exchanged a kiss.

"Thanks for coming to my first dinner party," Charmaine said, suddenly feeling shy all over again.

"We're happy to be here," Bea replied.

"It seems like we're finally turning a corner — all of us on Coral Island," Aidan said. "We're putting the pain of the past behind us and moving on. I don't think any of us understood how much having an unsolved murder hanging over our heads was impacting the community spirit. But it feels lighter to me. Has anyone else noticed?"

"Definitely," Evie replied. "I still miss my bookshop, but I'm feeling more hopeful."

"How is your brother?" Bea asked Charmaine, tentatively.

Charmaine inhaled a slow breath, steeling herself. The emotional reaction she felt whenever she thought about Sean was something she couldn't predict. Pain, fear, love, hope, frustration. She couldn't get a handle on what to think or believe. But her relief won out most of the time.

"He's admitted to the arson, so he's most likely going away for a long time."

"I'm sorry," Bea replied with a sympathetic look.

"I'm not," Charmaine said. "He burned your businesses to the ground — he's admitted it, so we know it for sure now. He deserves to be in prison for that. And honestly, my strongest reaction is relief because I know he can't hurt any of us any longer. Before he showed up on the island, I spent years worrying he'd find me, waiting and hoping he wouldn't. The fear was always there. Now, I can relax. He's not going to appear on my doorstep anytime soon. He'll be released one day, but I'll deal with that when it happens."

They finished eating, then carried bowls of dessert to the living room. When they were all seated in chairs and on the sofa, Bradford got down on one knee in front of Charmaine and pulled a small black box out of his jeans pocket.

Charmaine's heart skipped a beat. She pressed both hands to her mouth. There were gasps of surprise around the room.

"Charmaine, I'm so glad you're in my life. I still remember the first time I met you, so shy and quiet and yet there was something about you that drew me in. You're the most gentle, genuine person I know. I trust you with my heart and my life. I want to spend forever together. Will you marry me?"

There were cries of delight around the room as everyone watched on. Charmaine nodded her head furiously, and Bradford slipped a ring onto her finger. The small diamond sparkled and shone in the lamplight. It was nowhere near the size of the diamonds she'd given away to the police, but far more beautiful in her eyes. It represented love and hope for a future filled with joy.

Bradford stood to his feet and pulled her into his arms, lifting her off the ground to press to his chest. She kissed him and was lost in the happiness of the moment. Around them, the group cheered and clapped and embraced one another.

When Charmaine was back on her feet, one hand in Bradford's, she looked around to see tears gleaming in Bea's eyes and beaming faces everywhere.

Bea embraced her and whispered in her ear, "I finally have a sister, and I'm so happy it's you."

Twenty-Four

TAYA HAD a plane to catch and not a lot of time to prepare for the speech she had to give to the entire staff at the main office of Paradise Resorts in Blue Shoal. She slid her laptop into its case and slung her purse over her shoulder, then headed for the conference room.

In the room, she set her bags down and made her way to the end of the table by the projector. The entire room was packed. People sat in chairs around the long board table and stood in every spare centimetre of space — wherever they could.

"Thank you all for coming today," she said, spinning to face them.

She brought her fingers together briefly then let her hands fall to her sides. She'd expected to feel nervous, but she was surprised to find she was calm.

"As you all know, it's been a tough time not only for my family but for this business. We've lost the man who built everything you see around you from the ground up. And we'll feel that loss for a long time to come. I want to thank all of you for the support you've shown me as I get to know the business better and step into my father's shoes."

Her gaze panned the room, taking in the rows of serious faces — all attentive, all listening to what she had to say. She felt strong, responsible, confident. All these people relied on her; they had families who trusted her to not only keep their loved ones safe but to pay their wages every month. The magnitude of what her father had built and what now rested on her shoulders hit home in a new way. She couldn't let herself be overwhelmed by it; too many people needed her to step up and keep this business growing and thriving.

"I'll be visiting each one of our resort locations over the next twelve months. Andrew will be managing things here while I'm away, and I expect you to give him your full support."

She ran through her strategy for the next five years, giving them an overview of where she planned to take the company and inviting them to buy into her vision for the future. She watched as heads nodded around the room when she spoke of the potential for the business they were all part of and how they were a family first and foremost, who had each other's backs.

What she knew about the staff was that most of them had worked at Paradise Resorts for a long time. Staff turnover in the business was almost non-existent. When people got a job there, they stayed. If they wanted a promotion, they could travel to another resort location. And they often did, moving around the world, building their experience and their families, while remaining with the company. Her father had always encouraged it, saying *it's far better to invest in the employees you have than to put money into recruiting and training more.* She intended to continue that tradition and outlined her ideas for scholarships for educational opportunities, pathways to advancement, and increased leave allowances based on tenure. It was immediately apparent that the staff approved of her plans.

When she closed the meeting, there was a lot of smiling and excited chatter among the staff as they drifted away and back to their desks in groups.

Andrew walked over to meet her, a hesitant smile on his face. "Good speech."

"Thank you. How are your parents settling into life on Coral Island?"

"They're fine," he replied. "Still getting used to the language and cultural changes, but they love the beaches."

"I'm sure it will take a little time to adjust."

"I wanted to say again how sorry I am for how things went between us."

Taya's eyes narrowed. "Went between us?"

"You know, our relationship?"

"Oh, the way you broke up with me right after my father died? That's okay, I'm not upset about it any longer. I see it as a positive."

"I don't understand," he said, confusion darkening his eyes.

"I'm looking for someone to spend the rest of my life with. Someone who will stand by me through thick and thin. I want to marry a man who will love me no matter what and will defend me even if the people in his family criticise me. I must thank you for showing me now what kind of person you are, because I'm grateful we didn't take it any further. I would hate to have tied myself to someone who can't manage the most basic aspects of loyalty and love."

She pressed a fake smile to her face, turned on her heel, and strode for the door. She stopped at the door and looked over her shoulder.

"I hope you show more loyalty to the company, since I expect my employees to put this company ahead of their own feelings and I won't hesitate to make changes where they're needed."

He hesitated. "Uh... Of course."

"Great. I'll see you when I'm back in the office."

As she marched away down the hall, a real smile tickled her lips and she fought the urge to laugh out loud. It'd felt good to say the things she'd wanted to say. But she couldn't let it happen again. This was her workplace, and she intended to keep things professional. That meant no more dating anyone from the office. She wouldn't make the same mistake again.

* * *

As she sat in the airline's lounge several hours later, waiting for her international flight, Taya's phone rang. It was a video call from her mother. She answered the call with a tap and studied her mother's appearance.

"Mum, what are you wearing?"

Her mother trilled. "I'm going bowling. Can you believe it? I've bought this lovely lawn bowls outfit."

Mum panned the camera so Taya could see the entire thing. She blinked. "Um... Mum. That skirt is so short I can almost see your underwear."

"I know, isn't it cute? I've got my first game in a couple of hours, and I'm getting in some practice moves. Apparently, you have to bend down and sweep your leg to the side and, oh dear. I'm going to fall over; I can already tell. This is harder than it looks."

"Please don't fall. The last thing I need right now is for you to break a hip. I'm heading overseas for two weeks; you've got to stay safe and healthy at least until I get back."

Mum rolled her eyes. "You've become a bit bossy lately, sweetheart."

Taya huffed. "You've become..."

"What?"

"Never mind."

"No, go on. You can say it."

"A little young."

"You don't think I'm acting my age? Taya, that is such a nasty thing to say to someone. Didn't anyone ever teach you manners?"

There were so many retorts that popped into Taya's thoughts, but instead she knew the best way was simply to let it go. Maybe she was maturing after all.

"I'm sorry, Mum. You're right, that was rude. It's not up to me to police the way you act. You're a grown woman."

"Have been for a lot of years, my darling."

"I know... I feel very protective of you."

"And I appreciate that. But you've got to stop mother-henning me. I'm fine, honey. I don't need a mother; I need a daughter and a friend."

"You have me, I'm not going anywhere. Well, I am going somewhere, but only for work. I'll be back in two weeks."

"You mentioned that." Mum cocked her head to one side. "Dad would've been so proud of you."

"I hope so. I finally feel as though I can do this."

"Of course, you can. You've always had it in you, but sometimes we have to be thrown into the deep water before we learn to swim."

"So, you're joining a lawn bowls competition?" Taya grunted. "I never thought I'd see the day when my mother would put on an all-white uniform and go to a lawn bowls club."

"It's fun... Well, I think it'll be fun. Joan says they have a great time. And besides, we're going to coffee afterwards."

"That's more like it," Taya replied. "I knew there would be a reason."

"Coffee and cake. Gets me every time." Mum winked. "You have fun on your trip, my darling. I'll see you when you get back. Will you come to dinner that Friday night?"

"I'd love to. I'll be far too exhausted to cook and entirely sick of restaurant food."

"I'll make a pork roast."

"Sounds delicious."

"Camden and her boyfriend will be here too," Mum said.

"Will they? I don't think Camden told me about that..."

"No, it was a last-minute decision. We spoke about it early this morning when I went for my walk on the beach. I was showing her the sunrise and she said she missed it, so I asked why she doesn't come to visit."

"That's a great idea. Thanks, Mum. I miss her so much sometimes. I wish she'd move back here for good."

Mum leaned closer to her phone. "This is your chance. I'm making a nice meal, we'll put on some music, and bam, you offer her a job."

Taya laughed. "Really?"

"Why not? You *are* the boss, after all."

"Mum, when did you become so conniving? Or have you always been this way and I simply didn't recognise it?"

Mum poked out her tongue. "I'm off to bowling, love. Toodle-oo!"

Taya hung up the phone as her flight was announced. She slung her purse strap and laptop case over her shoulders and set off through the concourse to her plane. Would Camden work for her? She wouldn't answer directly to Taya, since she was a chef, she'd have to be in the kitchen of the Blue Shoal resort. But it would certainly mean Taya would see her more often. Still, she had a boyfriend and a life in Cairns. She might not want to leave all of that behind.

There was no harm in asking, though. If she said no, that was fine. Taya wouldn't hold it against her. But there was something special about this business being a place of family, and Taya wanted more than anything for Camden to be part of it. Mum clearly did as well. With a resolute heart, she boarded the plane, feeling more hopeful and alive than she had in years.

Twenty-Five

THE CHICKEN in the frying pan spat and hissed. Beatrice wiped her hands on her apron and set the lid on the pan. She switched off the potatoes, then drained and mashed them with butter and sour cream. Finally, she put them back in the empty pot with the lid on to keep them warm.

Her phone rang, and she pressed it to her ear with her shoulder as she worked.

"Hello?"

"Hey, Bea, you'll never guess what happened." Taya's voice was cheerful; it brought a smile to Bea's face.

"Really? What is it? Did you finally figure out how to be in two places at once, so we never have to miss you?"

Taya groaned. "Oh wow, that was corny."

"Okay, I'll try to do better next time. What is it? What's happened?"

"I offered Camden a job as sous chef at the resort here in Blue Shoal, and she said yes. She's going to give notice at her job in Cairns and move here within the month."

Bea pumped a fist in the air. "That's fantastic news! I'm so happy for you. What about her boyfriend?"

"She and Michael are working towards marriage, she told me."

"That sounds like an amazing plan. It's great to hear they're thinking about the future, unlike some." Bea couldn't help comparing Camden's future with Dani's. If things kept going the way they had been, Dani would end up spending the rest of her life with a man who didn't seem to have any plans to settle down or start a family and whose idea of high-class living was to have his girlfriend work at a cafe to help pay the rent on his flat full of cushions.

"Don't get down about the obnoxious professor, Bea. Dani is going to come to her senses. I know she will."

Bea walked into the living room and sat in an armchair with a sigh. "I don't know... I've always considered her sensible, responsible, mature. But these days, I feel like I don't know her at all. How can she think it's okay for her boyfriend to be almost twice her age and still he relies on her to pay half the rent on his flat. Where he lives, by the way, almost entirely without furniture or decor, other than his hookah. And Preston is no help at all, he and his new wife, seem to love Dani's professor. They invite him to dinner, and play tennis together. I still can't believe they live in our old neighbourhood and spend time with all our old friends."

"You have to let her live her own life. And forget about Preston and that country club neighbourhood. You're much better off."

"I know you're right, but maybe I have a responsibility to step in and tell Dani I don't like Damien and that he's not right for her."

Taya hesitated. "Well, I think you should say something. But maybe not that. Not in those words exactly. Be gentle. You know how stubborn Dani can be if she thinks you're overstepping."

"That's true," Bea admitted. She ran a hand through her

hair. "You're right, I can't say that. She'll spend her life with him to prove me wrong. So, what should I say?"

"Maybe you can point out how unsuitable he is, without speaking the words."

"That's a good idea." Bea thought about it for a moment. "I have no idea how to do that, but I'll come up with something." Her phone beeped. "Speaking of the devil, she's on the other line. That's such great news about Camden, honey. I'll talk to you later. Okay?"

She hung up on Taya then answered Dani's call with as warm a tone as she could manage. "How are you, sweetheart?"

"Mum, I'm on the island. I caught the ferry over. My battery was dead, but I charged my phone at Uncle Bradford's office. Can you please come and get me?"

* * *

Bea parked her car outside Bradford and Evie's office and hurried inside. She scanned the room and found Dani sitting huddled in a corner, with a backpack at her feet. Her eyes were red and swollen, and she looked miserable. Bea's heart sank, and she bustled across the room to wrap Danita up in her arms.

"Oh, sweetheart, what's happened? Are you okay? Why didn't you call me?"

Danita sobbed then drew a deep breath. "I'm sorry. I wanted to call, but I hadn't charged my phone and I didn't want to stop. I had to get out of there."

"You can tell me all about it in the car. Come on home, I'll make you a nice drink. I've got dinner already cooked."

She waved to Evie, who was busy with a customer, then headed out to the car, carrying Dani's backpack for her.

"What do you have in this thing, it weighs more than I do?"

Dani sniffled, then giggled. "My books. I'm a student, Mum. Remember?"

"Haven't you heard of the internet?" Bea grumbled beneath her breath as she readjusted the backpack on her aching shoulders.

"Damien says that the feel of pages at our fingertips helps ground us to the earth." After Dani sputtered the words, she burst into a howl of tears.

Bea helped her into the car, set the backpack in the boot, and then drove home. On the way, Dani stopped crying and stared out the window in silence. Bea glanced at her every now and then. She would give her space and time to open up. It never helped to push her daughter. Besides, she was home and that was what gave Bea some comfort. If Dani had called her in this state from Sydney, she would've felt anxious and helpless. But Dani was here, and she could comfort her, cook for her, give her a chance to work through whatever was going on in her life. She could be a mum, and that was Bea's favourite role.

They pulled into the garage, and Bea carried Dani's backpack inside. Aidan was in the kitchen, spooning dinner onto plates. He looked up, then gave Dani a hug, his eyes full of questions that Bea had no answers to.

She shrugged silently and he nodded.

"It's good to have you home," he said.

Dani sniffled. "It's good to be home. I missed you all so much."

"We missed you too. Let's sit outside on the deck to eat. It's so beautiful this time of night." Bea carried plates out to the table.

Aidan brought his own plate and a bottle of wine. They sat at the table and ate, discussing Dani's classes, Bea and Aidan's reunion, anything other than what was troubling Dani. The sun lit the ocean up like a bonfire, with red and orange streaks across the clear blue sky.

With a deep breath, Dani thrust her fork into a pile of mashed potatoes and then looked up at Bea. "I broke up with Damien."

Bea did her best not to grin or shout with delight. She was concerned about Dani and how her daughter felt, so instead she let that emotion shine through. "Oh, honey, I'm so sorry. What happened?"

Dani wiped her nose with her napkin. "He said I was immature and ridiculous."

"Why would he say that?" Anger flickered in Bea's gut.

"Because he thinks everything I do is wrong. He wanted me to quit uni so I could afford rent, but you didn't think it was a good idea and I agreed with you. I've got to finish uni, or I'll never get the kind of job I want. So, I stayed in class, and he wasn't happy about that. But then he said I should switch to architecture, because I was wasting my talent in design. When I investigated it though, it would've meant a lot more years of study and I'm not sure I even like architecture. So, I decided not to do it. There are a million other little things that I could tell you about, but this weekend, we went to a party at his friend's house. They were talking about politics, and I didn't agree with something one of them said, so I spoke up and told them. They were all super offended, and when we went home, he wouldn't even talk to me. The next day, we had a big fight about it and he said those things to me."

Bea bit down on her tongue. She glared at Aidan as if to say *can I call him names yet?*

Aidan shook his head. "I'm sorry, Dani. That sounds terrible."

"I know how much you liked him, sweetheart. But that's not a loving way to treat someone you are supposed to care about."

"I know," she said, fresh tears on her cheeks. "I told him that, and he said I was a baby. And if I was going to cry like a baby, I might as well leave. So, I did. And I gave up my flat to move in with him, so now I have nowhere else to go. I've neglected my friends to spend time with him and his friends, now I have no friends. I've been slacking on classes and assignments so I can work extra shifts to pay for his expensive rent, so my grades are falling. I've done everything I thought he wanted me to do, and all that's happened is I've lost myself. I don't even know who I am anymore, or what I want, or who I like spending time with. I've put all my energy into being more mature for him, and liking the things he does, and talking about the topics he's interested in, and he doesn't even appreciate it."

Bea put down her fork and reached for Dani's hand. She squeezed it gently. "You're learning some valuable lessons here, honey."

Dani blinked. "What? What lessons?"

"That you should never give up who you are to be with someone. You should be yourself, and if he loves you the way you are, then you can make a life with him. But don't ever change for him or hand over parts of yourself. Don't become another person or let go of your friends, your hobbies, or your career path for him. It won't work, and it'll leave you stranded."

She blew her nose, then nodded. "You're right. I won't do that again."

They finished dinner, then Bea served caramel pudding with vanilla ice cream for dessert. The sun had set by that time, and the mosquitos were out. So, they retreated into the house and put on the television. Dani sat with her legs over Bea's and held onto one of Bea's hands. She sniffled every now and then but otherwise didn't say a word. They watched some meaningless programs together, and Bea pondered how it'd come to this. All this time, she'd longed to tell Dani how little she and Damien had in common, that he wasn't right for her, that she should leave him and move on. But she'd held her tongue, for the most part, and now Dani had come to the same conclusion on her own. Besides that, she'd made a commitment to focusing more on her studies. It was everything Bea had hoped for.

"I'll have to find a new place next year when university is back in session, but for now I'm going to stay on the island and finish my classes online this semester. Do you think we could do something fun together this summer? "

Bea exchanged a look with Aidan. "I'd love to do that. What did you have in mind?"

"I don't know. I need some kind of adventure. I'm sick of working at the cafe, studying, and cleaning the flat. I want to do something that young people do. Damien never wanted to go out and do fun things. He was such a bookworm, not that there's anything wrong with that. But sometimes I like to go out and see things, try new foods, meet people, have adventures. And I've hardly ever done anything at all."

"I think it's a great idea," Aidan said. "You should go to Europe. See something of the world."

"Europe? Yes! I'd love that." Dani's grinned.

"We saw so many beautiful places. You'd love Italy... Oh, and Austria. Sweden was amazing, and the UK of course." Bea listed off some of her favourite destinations after the trip she and Aidan took together.

"We have six weeks; we could do a lot. Couldn't we?" Dani asked.

"We could fit quite a bit into six weeks. But it'll be winter, so we might have to include a ski trip," Bea said.

Dani clapped her hands together. "Can we please? I've wanted to go skiing for years and haven't been able to afford it."

"We'll all go, and we'll bring Harry and Grace too," Aidan said. "My treat."

Bea blew Aidan a kiss. "That sounds like the perfect adventure. Harry has two more years of study, so a summer in Europe will be just the break he needs. He's been working so hard."

"Grace is going to be over the moon too. She's looking forward to spending the summer together and she's never travelled overseas."

"There's something else I wanted to run by the two of you while Dani is here," Bea said.

Dani squeezed her hand. "What is it, Mum?"

"I've decided to finally go back to university. I know I've talked about it a lot, but I've never actually signed up. Aidan and I have discussed it, and I'm going to apply to study next year."

"What will you study?" Dani asked, her brow furrowed.

"Nutrition and food science," Bea replied. "I know it sounds like it's completely out of nowhere, but I want to study something I can do on the island. I'm never leaving Coral Island, so I need to get qualifications for a career I can do here. And I noticed there are no nutritionists on the island. I've already learned a lot about food and nutrition over the years, so I think it'll be a perfect fit."

Dani beamed. "That is amazing, Mum. You'll be great at that."

"Do you think so?"

"I know so."

Twenty-Six

THE BLUE SHOAL Inn glinted in the sunlight. Charmaine tented a hand over her eyes to drink in the vista. The quaint seaside inn with the brilliantly blue ocean and the blindingly white sand as a backdrop. It was like something out of a postcard. Too perfect to be real. And yet it was, and she was meeting her friends there for lunch.

Inside the inn, a kind concierge showed her to a private space behind the dining room with closed doors. The dining room was decorated with several pieces of art and an entire wall of glass doors that opened out onto a large deck. Inside the room, Taya, Bea, Penny, and Evie were huddled around a pram, goo-ing and gah-ing over Penny's baby.

"She's so adorable," Evie said.

"You're a champion, Penny. No complications, you were amazing," Taya said.

"Are you getting any sleep?" Bea asked.

"She's waking a couple of times per night, but otherwise, we're doing okay. Rowan has some time off work, so he's helping me manage by watching her so I can take naps during the day. I have no idea how I'm going to cope once he leaves on a trip."

Charmaine shut the door behind her, and they all looked up at once.

"Come and see Isla. She's a doll," Bea said.

Charmaine walked over to the pram and looked inside to see a tiny baby sleeping. Her dark lashes made half-moons on her pale cheeks, her lips were pink rosebuds.

"She's perfect," Charmaine whispered, in awe.

"I'm starving," Penny said. "We should eat before she wakes up because then I'll have to feed her instead of myself."

They all sat around a large, round table. A waitress took their orders and then brought them pitchers of lemonade and mineral water. Charmaine took a sip of lemonade; it was sweet and exactly what she needed. It'd been a long morning at the flower shop, and she was glad to get off her feet for an hour and have something to eat and drink.

"How are you going managing everything now without Betsy?" Taya asked.

"It's going well. There are a lot of things I didn't know about. Betsy managed most of the administrative and ordering side of things. But I'm getting the hang of it, and I've hired some part-time help. Which lets me do things like have lunch with friends."

"You're going to be fine," Bea replied. "You take everything in stride. You're strong and resilient."

Charmaine had never thought of herself that way before. In fact, if someone had asked her that question two years earlier, she would've stated without hesitation that she was too sensitive and didn't follow things through — because that's what she'd always been told, by her mother, by teachers, by everyone in her life. She was the tentative, shy, mousy girl who everyone overlooked and who ran rather than face any kind of hardship or conflict. But things had changed. She had changed. She wasn't that young, frightened girl any longer. She'd grown up, become a woman, and faced her fears.

"Thank you," she said. "I've finally grown some courage, I suppose."

"Definitely," Evie added. "After all you've been through, you can manage a flower shop without any trouble."

"I've got some news," Bea said as their meal arrived.

The waitresses placed everything on the table, and Bea waited until they'd left before continuing. "Aidan, Dani, Harry, Grace, and I are going to spend six weeks in Europe this summer. So, this will be our last girls' lunch for a while."

All the ladies exclaimed over that. Taya laughed. "Another trip? You only got back a few months ago."

"You're one to talk," Evie replied. "But seriously, Bea, is this how your life will be now? If so, I'm completely jealous."

"Ignore them." Penny spooned ravioli onto her plate. "I think it's a fantastic idea. You only live once."

"That's very true," Bea replied. "Besides when we get back, we'll be diving right into real life again. Aidan will be starting back up PE teaching at the primary school, and I've decided to go to university and study to become a nutritionist."

They all congratulated her, and Charmaine listened to their conversation in silence for several long minutes while she ate. The Italian-themed food was cooked perfectly and was delicious – her favourite was the veal parmigiana which melted in her mouth.

"Have you seen Hairy Legs again?" Bea asked Taya around a mouthful of carbonara.

Taya rolled her eyes. "We already established that his name is Brent. He's a forty-eight-year-old man, the least you can do is use his name. Besides, he's a cyclist and he shaves his legs. I bet you didn't know that."

Bea's eyebrows arched in surprise. "I can't believe you checked his leg hair."

Taya grunted. "I did no such thing... Oh fine, maybe I did."

They all laughed together. Taya pretended to be put out but soon laughed along with the rest of them.

"We're sorry, honey," Penny said. "We like him. He seems like he's grown into a wonderful man. Is he single?"

"He's divorced," Taya replied. "He married a woman from Peru, and it seems she never adjusted to life in Australia. She went back home and left him alone years ago. He's been single since."

"Poor guy," Bea said. "I know how that feels. Different situation, same result."

"So do you think you'll date?" Evie asked.

Taya couldn't keep the smile from her face. "He's already asked me out. He's flying in on the weekend, and we're going to dinner."

"Any date that involves airfare is pretty serious if you ask me," Evie said with a meaningful nod.

"We're going to take it slow," Taya replied. "I want to get to know him again. He was a sweet, romantic guy in high school, and I didn't appreciate that at the time. But I will appreciate it now."

"Amen, sister," Evie replied, raising her glass of water in a toast.

Meanwhile, Charmaine thought about her own future and where it might take her. She was still in shock that Bradford had proposed. She had to plan her own wedding, something she hadn't thought much about. It'd always seemed so impossible or, at the very least, unlikely. She'd fenced out everyone who cared about her in the past, so letting Bradford in had been difficult. But now being with him felt so right and so easy, she couldn't imagine life any other way.

Bea's words had resonated with her in a way she didn't expect. She was proud of Bea for choosing to restart her career, after losing her cafe. Charmaine had never gotten to finish her degree either, after her mother died, and had always assumed that part of her life was over, that she wouldn't get the chance to go back and try again. But maybe she could do it now that she had her own business and was earning decent money.

Did she want to study again? She wasn't sure. She loved working at the flower shop and planning events. But maybe she could see Bea's revelation as confirmation that she should keep reaching for her own dreams, whatever they might be or however impossible they seemed, like the art showing. It might not be a one-off, after all. Not if she worked at it.

Whatever she did, she'd have Bradford by her side and friends to keep her company on the journey.

"Thanks for letting me crash your girls' lunch," she said suddenly, interrupting their conversation.

Bea laughed. "You're very welcome, Chaz. After all, you may be twenty years younger than us, but you've become one of the girls."

"Definitely one of us now," Evie agreed.

"I'm sorry to break it to you," Taya added. "But you can't escape us now."

"You're a Coral Island institution — the Hilton family has lived here for generations. So, you're officially a local," Penny said. "You're one of us. Welcome to the Coral Island family."

* * *

Start a new series...

"**Love, love, love** these books!"

Ready to read start a brand new series? *The Waratah Inn* is Lilly Mirren's bestselling heartwarming women's fiction series. Buy the first book in this series!

Want to find out about all of my new releases? You can get on my VIP reader list by subscribing via my website, and you'll also get a free book.

Also by Lilly Mirren

WOMEN'S FICTION

CORAL ISLAND SERIES

The Island

After twenty five years of marriage and decades caring for her two children, on the evening of their vow renewal, her husband shocks her with the news that he's leaving her.

The Beach Cottage

Beatrice is speechless. It's something she never expected — a secret daughter. She and Aidan have only just renewed their romance, after decades apart, and he never mentioned a child. Did he know she existed?

The Blue Shoal Inn

Taya's inn is in trouble. Her father has built a fancy new resort in Blue Shoal and hired a handsome stranger to manage it. When the stranger offers to buy her inn and merge it with the resort, she wants to hate him but when he rescues a stray dog her feelings for him change.

Island Weddings

Charmaine moves to Coral Island and lands a job working at a local florist shop. It seems as though the entire island has caught wedding fever, with weddings planned every weekend. It's a good opportunity for her to get to know the locals, but what she doesn't expect is to be thrown into the middle of a family drama.

The Island Bookshop

Evie's book club friends are the people in the world she relies on most. But when one of the newer members finds herself confronted with her past, the rest of the club will do what they can to help, endangering the existence of the bookshop without realising it.

An Island Reunion

It's been thirty five years since the friends graduated from Coral Island State Primary School and the class is returning to the island to celebrate. A reunion can mean only one thing — Coral Island's secrets and lies will finally unravel and the truth will be revealed.

THE WARATAH INN SERIES

The Waratah Inn

Wrested back to Cabarita Beach by her grandmother's sudden death, Kate Summer discovers a mystery buried in the past that changes everything.

One Summer in Italy

Reeda leaves the Waratah Inn and returns to Sydney, her

husband, and her thriving interior design business, only to find her marriage in tatters. She's lost sight of what she wants in life and can't recognise the person she's become.

The Summer Sisters

Set against the golden sands and crystal clear waters of Cabarita Beach three sisters inherit an inn and discover a mystery about their grandmother's past that changes everything they thought they knew about their family...

Christmas at The Waratah Inn

Liz Cranwell is divorced and alone at Christmas. When her friends convince her to holiday at The Waratah Inn, she's dreading her first Christmas on her own. Instead she discovers that strangers can be the balm to heal the wounds of a lonely heart in this heartwarming Christmas story.

EMERALD COVE SERIES

Cottage on Oceanview Lane

When a renowned book editor returns to her roots, she rediscovers her strength & her passion in this heartwarming novel.

Seaside Manor Bed & Breakfast

The Seaside Manor Bed and Breakfast has been an institution in Emerald Cove for as long as anyone can remember. But things are changing and Diana is nervous about what the future might hold for her and her husband, not to mention the historic business.

Bungalow on Pelican Way

Moving to the Cove gave Rebecca De Vries a place to hide from her abusive ex. Now that he's in jail, she can get back to living her life as a police officer in her adopted hometown working alongside her intractable but very attractive boss, Franklin.

Chalet on Cliffside Drive

At forty-four years of age, Ben Silver thought he'd never find love. When he moves to Emerald Cove, he does it to support his birth mother, Diana, after her husband's sudden death. But then he meets Vicky.

An Emerald Cove Christmas

The Flannigan family has been through a lot together. They've grown and changed over the years and now have a blended and extended family that doesn't always see eye to eye. But this Christmas they'll learn that love can overcome all of the pain and differences of the past in this inspiring Christmas tale.

HOME SWEET HOME SERIES

Home Sweet Home

Trina is starting over after a painful separation from her husband of almost twenty years. Grief and loss force her to return to her hometown where she has to deal with all of the things she left behind to rebuild her life, piece by piece; a hometown she hasn't visited since high school graduation.

No Place Like Home

Lisa never thought she'd leave her high-profile finance job in the city to work in a small-town bakery. She also never expected to still be single in her forties.

HISTORICAL FICTION

Beyond the Crushing Waves

An emotional standalone historical saga. Two children plucked from poverty & forcibly deported from the UK to Australia. Inspired by true events. An unforgettable tale of loss, love, redemption & new beginnings.

Under a Sunburnt Sky

Inspired by a true story. Jan Kostanski is a normal Catholic boy in Warsaw when the nazis invade. He's separated from his neighbours, a Jewish family who he considers kin, by the ghetto wall. Jan and his mother decide that they will do whatever it takes to save their Jewish friends from certain death. The unforgettable tale of an everyday family's fight against evil, and the unbreakable bonds of their love.

MYSTERIES

White Picket Lies

Fighting the demons of her past Toni finds herself in the midst of a second marriage breakdown at forty seven years of age. She struggles to keep depression at bay while doing her best to raise a wayward teenaged son and uncover the identity of the killer.

In this small town investigation, it's only a matter of time until friends and neighbours turn on each other.

Cast of Characters

As the *Coral Island* series grows, the cast of characters does too. I hope this handy reference will help you keep them sorted!

* * *

Aidan Whitlock - former professional footballer, current primary school PE teacher.

Andrew Reddy - The new manager at *Paradise Resort*.

Annie Draper - Bea's friend from Sydney.

Beatrice Rushton - previously married and living in Sydney, now a resident of Coral Island.

Betsy Norton - Elderly, American, owns the florist shop.

Bradford Rushton - Bea's younger brother, owns a charter fishing company out of Airlie Beach.

Brent "Hairy Legs" - Chased Taya in high school.

Brett O'Hanley - Beatrice & Aidan's contractor.

Buck Clements - Rowan's step father and June's ex-husband.

Camden Futcher - Taya's adult daughter, training to become a chef in Cairns.

Cameron Eldridge - Taya's father and owner of *Paradise Resorts*.

Charmaine Billings - new resident of Coral Island, works at Betsy's Florals.

Damien Lachey - Dani's boyfriend, the professor and architect.

Danita Pike - Bea's adult daughter, lives in Sydney

David Ackerman - Principal at the Coral Island primary school

Elias Rushton - Bea's father, lives on Coral Island.

Emily Johson - Evie Mair's twin sister

Eveleigh (Evie) Mair - Owner of *Eveleigh's Books*, the book shop attached the *Bea's Coffee*.

Finn Edgeley - Watson, the cat's, official owner.

Frank Norton - Betsy's adult son and Samantha's father.

Fudge - Beatrice's pug.

Gareth Johnson - Emily's husband (Evie's brother in law)

Grace Allen - Aidan's teenaged daughter.

Harry Pike - Bea's adult son, lives in Sydney.

Henry St James - Penny's stepfather, married to Ruby St James.

Jacqui St James - Rob St James' estranged wife.

Janice - Evie's assistant at the bookshop.

Julian St James - Rob's young son.

June Clements - proprietor of the *Coral Cafe* & Rowan's mother.

Kelly Allen - Grace's mother & Aidan's ex-girlfriend.

Luella Rushton - Bea's mother, deceased.

Mary Brown - Penny's grandmother, murder victim.

Ms Gossamer - librarian in Kellyville.

Penny St James - Owner of the *Coral Island Wildlife Rescue Centre*.

Preston Pike - Bea's ex-husband, lives between Sydney & Melbourne.

Robert St James - Penny's brother, travels around to work in construction.

Rowan Clements - June Clements' son, journalist.

Ruby St James - Penny's mother.

Samantha Norton - Betsy's granddaughter & Frank's daughter.

Samuel Jay Gilmore - the name on Buck's California driver's license.

Sean Billings - Charmaine's brother.

Taya Eldridge - Owns the Blue Shoal Inn, is Cameron & Tina Eldridge's daughter.

Tina Eldridge - Taya's mother, married to Cameron.

Todd Futcher - Taya's former husband, deceased.

Watson - Charmaine's visiting cat.

About the Author

Lilly Mirren is an Amazon top 20, Audible top 15 and USA Today Bestselling author who has sold over one million copies of her books worldwide. She lives in Brisbane, Australia with her husband and three children.

She always dreamed of being a writer and is now living that dream. Her books combine heartwarming storylines with realistic characters readers can't get enough of.

Her debut series, The Waratah Inn, set in the delightful Cabarita Beach, hit the *USA Today* Bestseller list and since then, has touched the hearts of hundreds of thousands of readers across the globe.

Made in the USA
Monee, IL
26 February 2024

54131785R00121